Had to
BeYou

ALSO BY KERIS STAINTON

It Had To Be You

KERIS STAINTON

bookouture

Published by Bookouture in 2017

An imprint of StoryFire Ltd.
Carmelite House
50 Victoria Embankment
London EC4Y 0DZ

www.bookouture.com

ISBN: 978-1-78681-290-2
eBook ISBN: 978-1-78681-289-6

For my sister Leanne, who, while I was writing this book, kicked cancer's ass.

PROLOGUE

I'm in the park. It's a bright day – the sun is golden and warm – but raindrops are glinting on the grass and the black iron railings are shiny. A taxi whooshes past. I see him in the distance and I immediately know he's mine. Or, if he's not mine yet, he's going to be mine. He's walking towards me along the path, but he's not looking in my direction, he's looking over towards the row of shops opposite. I breathe in the scent of freshly cut grass, coffee from the Greek cafe, garlic and tomatoes from the pizza place with the flashing neon sign.

I'm not moving, I'm just watching, staring, and he still hasn't looked at me, but I know that he'll be happy when he sees me, I can feel joy bubbling up inside me. But not just joy: warmth and safety and love.

He turns away from the shops and sits on a bench – his long legs stretched out in front of him – and tips his head back, turning his face up to the sun.

And I walk towards him.

CHAPTER ONE

'Do you have a book about bodies?' the man says without actually looking up at me.

Behind the counter, I frown, trying to remember where I've seen one. 'I think there's a book about anatomy in with—'

'No.' His long fringe hides his face. He lowers his voice, even though there's no one else in the shop. 'Not like that. Bodies. Like… naked bodies.'

'Oh.' My cheeks heat as I realise what he means. 'Yes. They're actually just behind me here.' I point to the high shelves in the back corner and he heads in that direction, without looking up. I hope he doesn't crash into any of the display tables.

'I think there's a book about anatomy,' Henry whispers, mimicking me.

'Shut up.' I glance over at the customer, who has taken down one of the huge, glossy art books and is flicking through it on a nearby table, his body curled over it like a comma.

'Not quite as bad as the time that woman asked you for the clitoris book,' Henry says. 'But a good Level Three blush.'

I'm twenty-five years old. I really shouldn't still blush when someone says 'clitoris'. And the ridiculous thing is that Henry blushes every time he repeats the clitoris story and yet he does it anyway to tease me. (And he's twenty-six.)

'You're the one who heard "*Simply Jesus*" as "Simply Cheeses",' I say. I mimic him: 'Is it by Nigella Lawson?'

Henry snorts. 'That guy was so offended.'

'Not as offended as the pregnancy perv.' But that was because Henry had chased him out of the shop and he hadn't even properly fastened his trousers back up.

A few minutes later, today's probable perv passes us as he leaves, head still down, the bell on the door jingling behind him, but he seems to have remained clothed at least.

'I'd better go and check he's left that book as he found it,' Henry says.

'Ew. I'll make us a tea then.'

The kitchen isn't a kitchen at all, it's basically a cupboard at the back of the shop, so I carry on talking to Henry as I put the kettle on.

'You were in my dream last night,' I tell him, as I take my *My life is a romantic comedy (minus the romance and just me laughing at my own jokes)* mug out of the cupboard.

'Stop, Bea,' Henry says. 'I'm blushing.'

'Not like that,' I tell him, dropping a teabag into the mug. 'We were on the Tube, but you were driving it and I was up there with you talking to you, but you kept saying I was distracting you, so I said I'd drive and I did, but it wasn't a Tube any more then, it was a bus, but the windows were all steamed up and I couldn't see where we were going.'

'I think that means you feel like you have a lack of control in our relationship,' I hear Henry say.

'Seriously?' I poke my head out of the cupboard. 'I mean, that could actually make sense, but—'

Henry laughs. 'No! I think it means you ate the last of the good cheese when you were watching *Master of None* last night.'

I did do that, he's right. I roll my eyes. 'Very helpful. Thank you.'

'I have always wanted to drive a Tube, though.'

'I know,' I say. 'That's why we always sit at the front on the DLR.'

'We should do that this weekend. It's been ages.'

He heads back behind the desk so I can see him from the kitchen.

'You didn't have your usual dream then?' Henry asks. 'I thought you had that every night.'

He means my recurring dream. About a man in the park. Everyone knows about it. Everyone takes the piss out of me about it.

'Not last night, no,' I say. Even though I did. 'And I don't have it every night. Just most nights.'

Once the kettle's boiled, I open the fridge and find that we're out of milk. Again. Even though there's a big sheet of paper with 'Use the last of the milk? Buy more!' written on it (I wrote it and put it there), no one takes any notice. I don't understand it. If you use the last of the milk – and you know you have because you've managed to wash out the plastic bottle and put it in the recycling box – WHY would you not go and get more? I could understand it maybe if the shop was far away (although that would still be selfish, obvs) but it's practically next door. Next door but one, in fact. So it literally takes two minutes to get there and back.

'For fuck's sake,' I mutter.

'We should just start drinking it black,' Henry says. 'Lazy bastards.'

I leave the milk-less tea and grab my coat off the hook on the back of the door.

'Will you be all right on your own?' I ask. The shop's empty, but we always ask each other this, it's become a running joke.

'I think I'll probably manage,' Henry says, sitting down behind the counter and opening a copy of the *Observer* that Craig, who works weekends, has left behind.

It was raining when I got here an hour ago, but when I step out of the shop onto the street, I realise the weather's changed

completely. It's a little chilly, but the sky is clear blue and the sun
is bright. The road is wet and shiny and I take a couple of steps
back as a black cab whooshes past – the pavement's narrow here
and I've been splashed before.

The grocer's is quiet – I've missed the early rush and I'm
too early for the lunchtime rush. Zeta is behind the counter.
She's staring down at her phone, her thumbs flying over the
keyboard, but looks up at me and smiles. I head towards
the back of the shop for the milk, stopping to consider an
avocado and maybe some tomatoes for my lunch. But I've got
a Tupperware of pasta so I should leave them till tomorrow.
I grab an apple for myself and an orange for Henry and pay
Zeta. As I'm leaving, her boyfriend passes me and I turn back
and watch him pick Zeta up and swing her around. They're so
cute together, but Henry always says their PDA is enough to
make the fruit go off. I suspect he thinks they're cute too – I'm
convinced there's a romance-loving heart hiding somewhere
inside his cardigan – but he'd never admit it.

✳

'Split,' Henry whispers to me, gesturing subtly at the couple who
come into the shop just after lunch. 'Definitely.'

'Why?' I ask, looking over at them. The man is much taller
than the woman. He's wearing a leather jacket and he's got a mes-
senger bag across his body. The woman is wearing a tea dress over
leggings and yellow Converse, the same as mine. She's turning
the card carousel and he's reading the back of one of the popular
paperbacks, but I can't see which one.

'He rolled his eyes when she said she wanted to look at the
cards.'

'So? Maybe they've looked at cards in like ten shops already?
Maybe he's sick to death of cards.'

'But eye-rolling is aggressive. In a relationship.'

I roll my eyes and then grin. 'They seem cute.'

We always play this game when couples come into the shop – trying to predict whether they'll stay together or split up. We started playing it after a couple came in who seemed loved-up at first – she had her hand in the back pocket of his jeans, which I hate, but still – but then later he held up a copy of one of the arty 'anatomy' books and called 'Remember when yours looked like this, eh?' across the shop to her. When she came to pay for the Nicholas Sparks book she was buying, she said, 'Sorry about him. He's a prick.'

*

'What about this one?' today's woman says, holding a card out to the man.

'I literally couldn't give a shit,' he says, without looking up from his book.

'Oh,' I say. 'I think you're right.'

'Right?' Henry says. 'I kind of want her to chuck him right now.'

I smile. That's the only problem with this game: we never know who won, we never get to find out which of us was right.

'I don't understand being with someone who speaks to you like that,' Henry says, once the couple have left. She didn't buy the card. He bought the book.

'Maybe he's having a bad day and he's usually an absolute sweetheart,' I say. 'You never know.'

'Or if he treats her like that in public, what's he like in private?' Henry counters.

'Maybe we should've written her a note. Like, "you don't have to stay with him if he's always this mean".'

'We should just get cards printed up with "Dump him" on them,' Henry suggests. 'We could stick them in the books.'

'All the books?' I say. 'Bold.'

'We could make different cards,' Henry suggests, as he starts peeling his orange. 'Get them printed for all eventualities. You know, like "Maybe try deodorant".'

I wrinkle my nose on reflex. We have more than one customer who 'negatively impacts the odour of the store', as a secret shopper report once worded it. Right now, thanks to Henry, it smells of citrus and the woody cologne he wears.

'They wouldn't all have to be negative,' Henry continues, warming to his theme. '"Nice shoes" or "Great hair!" or "Yes, your kids are annoying, but all kids are annoying sometimes and you seem like a great mum".'

'Specific,' I say, smiling. 'Or maybe more cryptic? Like "Maybe not" or "Reconsider".'

'"Repent!"' Henry says so loudly that I the older woman who's been perusing the self-help section glances towards us with a worried expression.

'Maybe "You're doing amazing, sweetie",' I say. 'Because who doesn't want to hear that?'

Henry stares at me for a second, his eyes looking a little unfocused behind his glasses. 'I actually like that idea.'

I grin at him. 'Right? Not sure head office would approve though.'

'No,' he says. 'Bastards.'

'Bastards,' I agree, mildly. They're actually fine. We barely hear from them. The one customer leaves. Henry goes to make us another cup of tea.

CHAPTER TWO

Henry and I walk home from work together, but when we get back to the flat he heads straight into his room, like he always does. After a day in the shop, I always want a beer or a glass of wine and a chat with one of our other housemates, but Henry seems to need at least a half hour alone to decompress. I'd found it weird at first, but I'm used to it now.

'Someone left the breakfast dishes again,' Freya says from the sink, her back to me.

'How did you know I was here?' I ask her, stopping behind her and resting my chin on her shoulder.

'I didn't know it was you. I just knew it was someone. And someone left the breakfast dishes again.'

That's the main downside about all of us sharing a kitchen – people don't do their dishes and sometimes they nick other people's food. Between home and work, I spend way too much time stressing over other people's bad kitchen manners. We take it in turns to cook most nights and it works out really well, but the dishes are a constant problem. Henry's been trying to talk his dad, who's our landlord, into getting us a dishwasher, but nothing doing so far.

I kiss Freya on the cheek and say, 'Leave them. I'll do them.'

'I'm nearly done now,' she says. 'Get a drink.'

The kitchen and the bathroom were the only rooms we were all meant to share when I first moved in here. There are five other rooms – it's a three-storey flat above a cafe in a Victorian terrace – and when I moved in they were all occupied. Freya and I both have back rooms. Even though it's his dad's place, Henry has a really tiny room next to the front door. When I moved in, Adam and Celine were in one front room and Henry's cousin was in the other. After he'd gone, we interviewed a few people, but didn't like anyone and finally realised that we just didn't want anyone new, so Henry's dad said we could all pay a bit extra in rent and convert the upstairs bedroom into a lounge. It was the best thing we ever did.

'What are you making?' I ask Freya, as I grab myself a bottle of Corona from the fridge.

'Corned beef hash.'

'Perfect,' I say, shoving one of the dining chairs back against the wall so I'm out of the way. I sit down and stretch my arms over my head, feeling my back stretch and my spine click. Even though the shop's not busy, I spend most of my time standing and it's always good to sit down when I get home. The beer helps too.

The front door slams and Celine bursts into the kitchen, throwing her bag down on the table and yanking her jacket off.

'Is Adam home?'

She hangs her jacket – caramel suede, expensive – over the back of one of the chairs, then runs her hands through her long dark hair. I didn't think I'd like Celine when I first met her and I absolutely admit it's because she's so gorgeous. And smart – she's a lawyer specialising in copyright. She's totally intimidating. But she's also lovely and funny and kind and I'm an idiot. She'd actually be the perfect housemate if it wasn't for her and Adam's rows. And then the making up. The making up might actually be worse than the rows – Freya, Henry and I have discussed it, but we're undecided.

I shake my head. 'Don't know. Only just got home.'

'I haven't seen him,' Freya says, turning from the sink to the cooker.

'Ugh, he's such an arsehole,' Celine says. She opens the fridge, gets a beer and almost breaks the wall-mounted opener she smacks it so hard.

'Bad day?' Freya asks, stirring the contents of a pan with a wooden spoon.

'Bad fucking life,' Celine says. She takes a long swig of her beer then says, 'I think it's over this time.' She peels her false eyelashes off and drops them into her bag.

'Why?' I ask. I'm not worried. She's said it before. Loads of times.

She shrugs. 'He's been ignoring me all day even though we've talked about him doing that before. He knows I hate it. I don't care if he tells me he hasn't got time to talk, but he needs to *tell* me that, not just ignore me!'

'What if he, ah, hasn't got time to tell you?' Freya asks.

I bite the inside of my mouth to stop myself from laughing.

'Listen, if he's got time to go to that fucking noodle place with his dickhead mate at lunchtime, he's got time to text me. Knob.'

She opens the fridge, pulls out a head of lettuce, a packet of tomatoes and a red pepper, drops them onto the dining table and starts making a salad in an incredibly aggressive way, the knife screeching against the glass chopping board.

'Would you rather peel the potatoes?' Freya says. 'I'm not sure the lettuce can survive that kind of abuse.'

Celine puts the knife down and crunches into a slice of pepper.

'Should it be this hard?' she says, looking at me and then Freya and back to me again. 'I don't know if it should be this hard.'

'The pepper?' Freya says.

'Come on,' Celine says. 'I'm really asking.'

Freya and I look at each other. Celine and Adam fight all the time, but Celine's never asked our opinion before.

'I think it's hard for a lot of people,' I say, tentatively.

'Is it hard for you?' She stares at me and I realise how tired she looks. She's got grey smudges under her eyes and her skin looks almost translucent.

'I don't have a boyfriend,' I say. 'I haven't had one for... a while.'

'I know, but, I mean, in the past. Has it been hard? Did you fight?'

I shake my head. 'I, um, no? Not really. But only because I've never really had a proper relationship. I've never really lived with anyone or even...' I drink some of my beer, but my chest feels tight. I don't really want to talk about this.

Celine frowns. 'What about you?' she asks Freya.

'I don't know,' Freya says. 'I think it's different with girls? Or maybe it isn't, I don't know. But I like the fighting and the fucking, you know? I like a passionate relationship.'

Celine smiles for the first time since she came home. 'We do enjoy making up, it's true.'

'Sometimes repeatedly,' Freya says, holding the spoon out towards Celine. 'Taste this.'

Celine takes some food off the spoon. 'That is really good.'

'Don't put it back in the—' I start to say, but the spoon's back in the pan before I can even finish.

'Celine hasn't got any germs, have you?' Freya says. 'She's perfect and pristine. I'd be honoured to have a bit of her spit in my dinner.'

'Ugh,' I say. 'You're the worst.'

'I'm taking my perfect, pristine self for a shower,' Celine says, putting her beer down on the table. 'If Adam comes back, tell him I've left him and see what he says.'

*

'There's a new guy at work,' Freya tells me, once Celine's gone. 'And he is right up your alley.'

'Ugh,' I say. 'No thanks.'

Freya turns from the stove and just stares at me, her eyes narrowing, until I say, 'God. What?'

'He's a writer—'

'He works with you? So he's actually a teacher.'

She shrugs. 'You can be both. He's published.'

Against my better judgement, this actually intrigues me. 'What has he published?'

'A novel. For children. Something to do with video games? And I think he said weasels? But the bell went, so I might have got that wrong. He said it was Book of the Month in Waterstones. Or Smith's. He's writing the sequel now. Anyway, he's cute. And he reads. He was reading at lunch.'

'A novel?'

She nods. 'By David Nicholls. But not the film one.'

'*Us*? *Starter for Ten*?'

'Dunno. I only noticed the name. But he basically writes romance, right? For boys?'

I nod.

'So!'

'So what?'

'He's single, I checked.'

'You're suggesting I go out with a man just because you saw him reading a boy romance?'

'And he writes!'

'Yeah, I'm going to need more than that.'

'Right,' Freya says. 'And that's exactly your problem.'

'What's my problem?'

'You're too fussy.' She turns her back on me while she lifts lids off pans and stirs stuff.

'I don't think I'm fussy!' I say, pausing to drink some of my beer. We've had this conversation before, albeit not for a while.

Freya snorts. 'Oh please. You wouldn't go out with Neil because he said "fillum".'

'It wasn't "fillum", it was "chimley". And that wasn't the reason. I saw him picking his nose with his glasses.'

'Oh yeah,' she says, replacing the lids and turning round to look at me. 'He does that. But, you know, everyone's got bad habits, you just have to beat them out of them.'

I sigh, heavily.

'I know what you're thinking,' she says. 'And you're kidding yourself.'

'What?' I pick at the label on my lager.

'Dream Man is only perfect because he doesn't exist. If he did and you ever actually met him, you'd learn that he has skiddy pants and picks his feet and doesn't know which is Khloé and which is Kourtney—'

'*I* don't know which is Khloé and which is Kourtney.'

'Seriously? Khloé's really tall and—'

'And I don't care,' I interrupt.

Freya pulls a face. 'You know Kim, right? That's the most important thing. Actually, did you see the thing about…'

She starts telling me something she read about Kim Kardashian's new baby – or that she's going to have another baby, I'm not sure – and I congratulate myself on a successful subject change. It's not usually quite that easy to shift Freya's focus. Particularly when it comes to my lack of love life.

*

After dinner – we had to turn up the music in the kitchen to drown out Adam and Celine's shouting while we ate Freya's corned beef hash – I go to my room and read one of the new romance novels from the delivery today until my eyes are closing and I'm reading the same line over and over. I take a break to download the sample of the latest David Nicholls (I've read *One Day*, but nothing else) and then switch off my light. It's not even ten o'clock.

I'm almost asleep when I hear low moaning coming from downstairs. I groan and roll over, pressing my face into my pillow. Great. No chance of me getting to sleep for a while yet then.

'Oh god, yes. There. There. Yes.'

I bang my head on my pillow.

'No! There!' Celine shouts. 'Not there. No. No! There!'

Celine lets out a low moan and I clamp my hands over my ears and try to do what I've done to help me get to sleep for years now: tell myself a story. For as long as I can remember, I've daydreamed before going to sleep. I'm not a big daydreamer during the day, but I always like to have a little story to tell myself when I get into bed. I think I can even remember the very first one. We were on holiday in Cornwall, staying in a static caravan that belonged to someone Dad knew from the pub. We went out on a boat trip around the bay and the guy who owned the boat was really cute. I remember Dad teasing me about how smitten I was and I got annoyed 'cos I was embarrassed. But then in bed that night, I told myself a story about being out on the boat again, but just me. And the guy had fallen overboard and I'd had to leap in to save him. And that was it. I'm not even sure there was any kissing. Just that he needed help and I saved him and it felt good.

'Shit! Ow, no. That's my hair. You're on my hair!'

As I got older, the dreams definitely started to include kissing. And sometimes more, but usually not because the set-up was so involved that I fell asleep before I got to any sex business. The dreams almost always involved a celebrity or a character from a TV show or film. After watching *Friday Night Lights*, Tim Riggins kept me busy for months. Sometimes I'd get something wrong in the set-up – dream me would say something real me would never say, or someone else would do something annoying or out of character – and I'd have to go back to the beginning. Over the years, I've come up with a series of concepts that always work, no matter who the leading man is: sitting next to a stranger on a plane who turns out to be someone super hot. Or trapped in a lift. Or on holiday on a tropical island where the super hot guy just happens to be on holiday alone, recovering from heartbreak. They're all flexible, all reliable. I don't know if anyone else does this. I hope so. I've no idea how anyone gets to sleep otherwise.

'Oh yeah,' Adam groans. 'Go on. Go on! Go on!' He sounds like he's encouraging a horse.

But once I started having the park dream – the recurring dream I've been having for ten years now – that was the thing I thought about before bed the most often. I would relive the actual dream and then embellish it a little. We'd have a picnic. Or we'd be kissing on the bench. Or I'd be in the park waiting for him and would see him in the distance and know he was coming to meet me. Or he'd be on the bench alone and I'd be late and watch him for a while, knowing he was waiting for me, knowing how happy he'd be when I got there, knowing we were in love and happy together. Once I pictured us arriving at the same time at opposite sides of the park and running to meet each other, but that one was too cheesy even for me.

Adam is making a high-pitched squeaking noise, so I scrunch my eyes up and try to focus on the park dream. I'm in the park… And he's on a bench…

'Oh fuck!' Celine shouts. 'Oh shit!'

'Get in!' Adam shouts.

And then they're both mercifully quiet. I think about the park dream and slide one hand down between my legs.

CHAPTER THREE

I'm in the park.

The sun is shining and he's walking towards me along the path, looking over at the row of shops opposite. A bus passes, an advert for a Reese Witherspoon romcom on the side, and he glances back over his shoulder.

He still hasn't looked at me, but I know that he'll be happy when he sees me. I want to run over to him, but I make myself wait.

He turns away from the shops and sits on a bench, his long legs – in black jeans – stretched out in front of him – and tips his head back, turning his face up to the sun. And I walk towards him…

✳

And then I wake up. As I always do. As I always have. Every single time I've had this exact same dream for the past ten years. Occasionally one of the details changes. Once he left the park and crossed the road and went into a shop that's not actually there. He looked at the sandwiches. I followed him. But I still didn't approach him or speak to him.

Once a squirrel ran up to the bench and he reached down and gave it a nut. Why he'd be carrying nuts I don't know.

Another time I got almost right up to the bench – so close I could see his face. Except I couldn't see it, the sun was too bright and it dazzled me. I cried when I woke up from that one.

But last night's was the basic, standard dream I've been having all these years. The one I think of as the main story – squirrels and sandwiches are sort of like DVD extras, nice to know but not actually essential to your enjoyment of the plot. He is the main story. The man of my dreams.

*

'You know that scene in *When Harry Met Sally* where Sally tells Harry about her recurring sex dream?' Freya says, as she slides a coffee across the dining table towards me.

'Yep.'

'And she says that a faceless man rips off her clothes? And Harry thinks it's really dull?'

'Yes.'

'Your dream's way worse than that.'

I roll my eyes as Freya grins at me. Freya thinks my dream is boring and pointless. She can't believe I've been having the same, according to her, 'dull as fuck' dream for ten years. And I can't make her understand that it's not what happens in the dream that's important – because I agree it's not that exciting – but the way it makes me feel.

'Wanna hear my dream?' Freya asks. She drinks some of her own coffee and then gets up and opens the fridge. She takes a packed lunch to work every day.

'Not really.'

She ignores me. Of course.

'I dreamt I was on a jet-ski and Gina Rodriguez was waving to me from a yacht. I drove up to the yacht and a door opened in the side and a wave, like, swooped me into the yacht and when I got up on deck Gina was waiting for me. In a bikini.'

'That's the gayest dream you've ever had.'

She grins at me over her shoulder. 'Not even. It was a good one though. But you know what, if I'd been having that dream for ten years I still wouldn't be happy. Not unless it progressed. Not unless I got her out of her bikini. Or, like, Beyoncé turned

up or something. The same boring ass dream over and over again?'
She flicks her hand.

'I don't find it boring though, that's the point. It's comforting.'

'What's comforting?' Henry says as he walks in.

Me and Freya are still in our night clothes. I'm wearing proper
button-up pyjamas with clouds on them. Freya's in knickers and
a vest. Henry always gets fully dressed before he comes out of
his room. I've seen him in hoodies and trackies, but never in
whatever he wears at night.

'Bea's boring dream, apparently,' Freya tells him.

'Put something on, will you?' he says, as he always does. 'Puts
me off my breakfast.'

'Stop oppressing me,' Freya replies, bending down to get
Tupperware out of the cupboard.

Henry turns away so fast I'm surprised he doesn't hurt himself.
When he looks at me, his cheeks are pink. Freya totally does it
on purpose.

'You had the dream again?' he asks me.

I nod over the top of my mug.

'I was telling her that her obsession would be more under-
standable if the dream progressed,' Freya says, pulling a packet
of Frazzles out of the cupboard. 'If, like, she straddled him on
the bench or something.'

'And I was saying I find the repetition comforting,' I say. 'Like
how you can watch a favourite film over and over and love it just
as much.'

'Like *Inception*,' Henry says.

'Yes. Except I haven't seen *Inception*.'

Henry shakes his head. He's appalled at my lack of interest in
Christopher Nolan films.

'But like *Pretty Woman*. I couldn't even tell you how many
times I've watched it. I know exactly what's going to happen. But
if it's on TV, I have to watch it. No question. And I don't have

to worry it's going to have a sad ending or a horrible ending, I know it all works out.'

'And they all lived anti-feministly ever after,' Freya says.

'It's not anti-feminist,' I argue, pushing my chair back from the table. I need to go and have a shower. 'They rescue each other.'

Freya blows a raspberry.

✻

In the shower, I think about what Freya said. I know she thinks I'm ridiculous for obsessing over the dream. But I've been having it for ten years for a reason. I've never had any other recurring dreams. I dream a lot, but I've never had another dream that feels as real as this one. So I don't care that Freya thinks it's boring or that I'm ridiculous for believing it will come true, because it has to. Otherwise what's the point?

CHAPTER FOUR

'We're out of milk,' Henry calls from the kitchen in the shop.

'For fuck's sake!' I mutter, before I remember that we used the last of it yesterday and I said I'd pick some up this morning on the way in and then totally forgot.

'I'll go out in a bit,' I call back and carry on scrolling the intranet for price and promotion changes. If I don't do that first thing it doesn't get done and it's one of the main things head office get worked up about. Once that's done, and I've checked the bags, till roll and tidied the bookmarks, I tell Henry I'm popping out.

'Will you be all right on your own?' I call from the door.

'I think I'll manage,' he says, without looking up from the Neil Gaiman novel he's reading from stock.

*

The weather's much nicer than yesterday – the sun's shining in a half-hearted, watery way that always makes me feel weirdly positive. I'm not sure if I have some associated memory (that I can't actually remember), but this weather makes me feel like I can do anything. But I can't really. All I can do is buy milk and take it back to the shop. At least I can make a tea for me and Henry – that I can do.

And there's something else I can do. I can go to Tesco. We love the Greek grocer's, but Tesco is much cheaper and we have been told to keep an eye on petty cash. And that way I can go through the park. If Henry looks out of the shop window, he'll wonder where I'm going, but I trust he's engrossed enough in his book not to notice. Plus the glass is covered in brightly coloured promo stickers so it doesn't exactly give the best view.

I walk over the zebra crossing towards the cinema and then I keep going. There's something about London in the sun. Particularly this bit of London. It's so unchanged – if it wasn't for the cars and the signs and the bus stops and the dustbins, it could be a hundred years ago. Maybe two hundred.

I keep walking until I'm almost at the square and I tell myself I'll just have five minutes there and then I'll get the milk – and maybe some biscuits or pastries. Henry loves a chocolate twist. I open the gate and step into the gardens. Someone is sitting on the bench on the left, but as I get closer I see it's an old woman, a small dog in a bag at her feet. It's not the right bench anyway. I keep walking. I walk all around the path, trying not to look directly at the bench, but I can't really help it – my gaze just drifts there automatically now.

I'm almost back at the gate when I get that weird déjà vu feeling. I'm used to it, it happens quite often, but this time it's such a strong sensation that it actually makes me feel a bit dizzy. It feels like the ground is tilting underneath me and I wonder if I might be about to faint. That would be embarrassing. I reach out and steady myself against a tree. The feeling of the bark under my hand – rough and dry but also mossy – is familiar too. I know the next thing I need to do is to turn around. I would always look back when I get to the gate anyway, but I need to turn around now. I turn. And there he is.

He's sitting on the right bench, halfway down the side where I just walked. He must have been behind me because he definitely wasn't there when I passed. Everything about him is exactly as I expected it to be: black boots, jeans, a black T-shirt and a black pea coat, rectangular black glasses. His dark hair is swept back from his forehead and his face is turned up to the sun. I lean against the tree and stare at him. I know he doesn't look over because I've seen this before. I know I can just watch him, that he'll sit there, head back, eyes closed, legs crossed at the ankle.

I've waited for this moment for so long that I thought it would feel much weirder than it does. It actually seems completely natural. I don't even feel particularly nervous. In fact, I'm almost giddy with happiness, so much that I almost want to laugh out loud. How many times have I walked up to this park to look for him? How many times have I talked about this to my friends? It's become a running joke now. They won't believe I've really seen him.

I stand up straight. Actually, they really won't believe it. They'll think I've completely lost the plot. Even more than they did when I told them about him in the first place. I sneak my phone out of my pocket and scroll to the camera. I'm not close enough to get a good photo, I know, but anything's better than nothing. I zoom in slightly – too much and it will be blurry, the camera on this phone isn't great. Just as I tap the screen to take the photo, he looks up. He looks up and over at me. I hear myself gasp and before I even think about it I'm out of the park and walking up towards the shops. I put my phone back in my pocket with shaking hands. He wasn't supposed to look at me. He wasn't supposed to see me. That wasn't meant to happen. Shit.

But then I realise I need to go back. I need to talk to him. I've waited so long and there he is, I can't just run away, can I? What if I never see him again? I think about what Freya said this morning about walking over and mounting him. Of course I'm not going to do that, but maybe I could go over and just talk to him. Yes. That's what I should do. Oh god.

I turn back towards the park, muttering 'Please still be there… please still be there…' under my breath as I walk. He is still there, I can see him as soon as I get to the corner. I should plan what I'm going to say, but I can't think – all my brain power seems to be concentrated on getting me into the park and across to his bench. And then I'm there. He's sitting in the centre of the bench, so I drop down next to him and stare straight ahead.

'Hi,' I say, eventually.

Out of the corner of my eye, I see him turn his head very slightly towards me and I hold my breath as if that's going to make me invisible. I dig my fingers into the bench under my thighs to keep myself rooted and stop my hands from shaking.

'Hey,' he says. His voice is deep. I knew it would be.

'I know this is weird,' I say. 'I'm sorry.'

He laughs. He's got a nice laugh. 'No, it's OK. But I'm just gonna tell you right now that I'm not interested in learning about The Lord.'

He's got a bit of an accent, but I can't quite place it. Midlands, maybe. It throws me (and I was already fairly well thrown). I turn to look at him. He's really handsome. Like stupidly handsome. There is no way I would have been brave enough to speak to him under normal circumstances.

I smile. 'No, sorry. I don't want to. I'm not one of those… I'm not religious. At all. I just… I saw you and… I had to come and talk to you. That makes me sound mad, I know, but I'm not. Honest.'

'It's OK,' he says again. 'I like a girl with balls.'

I laugh.

He grins. 'I don't mean with actual real balls.'

'No, I wouldn't have thought so.' Are we having a conversation? I think we're having a conversation.

'I mean, I like that you came over to talk to me.'

'I'm glad,' I say. 'I know it's a bit of a weird thing to do.'

'Nah,' he says, tipping his face up to the sun again. 'I was just wishing I had someone to share this with. You have perfect timing.'

'Share what?' I ask.

'The word of The Lord.'

I almost groan out loud, but then I notice that he's grinning. 'Sorry,' he says. 'Couldn't resist.'

We sit in silence for a minute or two. I'm desperately trying to think of something to say that doesn't make me sound completely demented, but I'm struggling. Eventually I say, 'So do you come...' I realise almost too late that I'm about to ask him if he comes here often. No. '... to this park a lot? I don't think I've seen you before.'

He pulls a face that makes his mouth turn down at the corners. It's adorable. 'Not a lot, no. And I don't think I've seen you before either. I would've noticed.'

I stretch my legs out in front of me and look at my ankle boots. My purple tights.

'Do you work near here?'

He shakes his head. 'I've got an interview. Just over there.' He gestures towards the far side of the park. 'Just trying to, you know, sort my head out.'

'Oh right,' I say. 'Sorry to disturb you then. I'll let you...'

'Nah, it's OK,' he says. 'If my head's not sorted now, it's probably too late, to be honest. Do you work nearby?'

I nod. 'Just round the corner. In the discount book shop.'

'Cool.'

'Yeah. It is. Sort of.'

He's smiling at me and I can't think of anything to say. I need to think of something good. Something intriguing or alluring. Something that'll make him ask me out.

'I've just come out for milk,' I say instead. For fuck's sake.

He shuffles on the bench as if he's making a move to get up and I can't let that happen. I just can't.

I take a deep breath. 'Do you want to – maybe – get a coffee some time?'

He grins at me. His teeth are so straight. And white. 'Sounds good. When's good for you?'

'Tomorrow?' I say. Even though I want to say today. Even though I want to forget about work and for him to forget about the interview and for us to go right now.

He takes his phone out of his pocket and I tell him my number. He keeps looking at me and I finally realise why.

'Oh! Bea! I'm Bea. Bee, ee, ay.'

'Nice to meet you, Bea,' he says, holding out his hand. 'I'm Dan.'

CHAPTER FIVE

'You're not going to believe what happened to me today,' I say, as I walk into Freya's room after work.

'Someone wanking in the pregnancy section again?' she says from her chair in the corner.

'Oh my god. No. Something good.'

'Cool, just a sec,' she says, holding up one finger. She's got her legs curled up underneath herself and an exercise book on her knee, pen in hand. There's a huge pile of similar books on the small round table next to her. I still can't believe how much work she has to bring home with her, but she tries to get it done as soon as she can, so the rest of the evening's her own.

I sit on the end of her bed and look around her room.

Freya's room is like something from an interiors magazine and it always surprises me. My room still basically looks like a student room. Or my bedroom at home. *Home* home. But Freya has pictures and mirrors and a beautiful multicoloured blown-glass chandelier.

'Is that new?' I say without thinking, spotting a red glass vase on the window ledge. The light's shining through it and reflecting on the black and white rug.

'Shush,' she says, without looking up.

I shuffle off the bed and walk over to look at her photos. One full wall is covered in them, all individually displayed in frames Freya picks up in charity shops and jumble sales and only very occasionally IKEA. I look at the photo of her mum in the seventies, wearing a pair of short shorts and perched on the back of a moped; Freya's brother as a baby wrapped in a blanket but with a pair of heart-shaped sunglasses perched on his head; the dog she had as a kid, lying across her bare feet.

Before I reach the photos of me and Henry, Celine and Adam, Freya says, 'Done. This one managed to confuse Elizabeth I and Elizabeth II which is quite impressive. "The Virgin Queen is mother to four children…" Work needed on history *and* sex ed.'

I flop back on the bed again. Her mattress is so much softer than mine.

'I found him,' I say.

'Who him?' She uncurls her legs, sticking them out straight in front and circling her ankles. 'Not *him* him?'

I swing myself up to sitting and nod. 'In the park. I went to get milk this morning and stopped for a look and he was there. He looked exactly the same.' I hold my phone out to show her the photo, but it's not great. My hands were shaking too much to get a clear shot.

'Wow.' She looks at it and then at me.

'I asked him out. And he took my number. We're going for coffee tomorrow.'

'Wow,' she says again. She doesn't look impressed.

'What?'

'I just…' She twists her mouth to one side and I've known her long enough to know what that means. 'You don't really think it's him, right?'

'Of course it's him.' It is. It must be.

She reaches for her drink on the table behind the exercise books, gulps some and puts it back. 'I get that you think it's him. Because you've wanted this for so long. But I don't want you going out with some random bloke you picked up in a park because you think you've been dreaming about him, you know?'

I shake my head. 'I know. But... it really is him. Everything was the same. Even his name. I knew his name was Dan—'

'You didn't know his fucking name was Dan. You've literally never mentioned that before.' She's looking at me like I've lost my mind.

'No. I didn't know before. But as soon as he said it I knew.'

'Can you hear yourself? You sound insane.'

'I know that,' I tell her. 'I'm not stupid. And I know you don't understand. But I know the dream and I know it was him.'

She closes her eyes and rolls her head from side to side. 'I'm sorry,' she says, opening her eyes and staring straight at me. 'I know it means a lot to you. And maybe it really was him, what the fuck would I know?'

'It was him,' I say. 'I know it was.'

'I just want you to be careful,' she says.

'I know,' I tell her. 'We're only going for a coffee. I won't go anywhere with him. And I'll ring you after.'

'That's not what I meant,' Freya says. 'OK.' She pulls her legs up under her again. 'My first work placement, I met a woman. She was older than me, she'd been working there about three years, I think. She had a daughter. She brought her in one day, she was gorgeous. One Friday night after work a bunch of us went to the pub for a quick drink and it turned into a late one. I was sitting next to her and we were talking and she told me her marriage was over. That her husband wasn't interested in her any more. That they were only staying together because of the baby. Her knee was pressing against mine under the table and I couldn't think straight because I just desperately wanted to kiss her.'

She tips her head back again, staring up at the ceiling.

'I didn't kiss her. And she didn't kiss me. We both went home and on Monday we went back to work and we never talked about it again. But I kind of got obsessed with her. I used to watch her all the time at work. We were on staggered lunches and I made sure I had the same break as her 'cos I thought when she and her husband did actually split, I'd be there. I'd be the one she'd come to, you know? I stalked her on Facebook. I looked up her address at work and went and sat in her local pub just in case she popped in. I thought she was The One, you know? And I don't even believe in The One. And then one day – this had been going on for months, like… six months? – and then one day her husband came to pick her up from work. And he kissed her and I stood and watched them, like the creepy stalker I was. He had his hand on the back of her neck and it killed me, it was so casually intimate. And I went home and got absolutely hammered.'

'God,' I say. 'I'm sorry.'

She shakes her head. 'The thing is, I realised – eventually, not immediately – that it wasn't about her at all. I was lonely. And insecure. And I felt out of my depth at work. And I just took all these emotions and feelings and pasted them onto her. I wanted her to save me. I'm not sure she even knew my name.'

It's only then that I realise the point of her story.

'You think this is about Anthony?'

She nods.

'It's not,' I say, standing up. 'It's nothing to do with him.'

'Don't go,' she says. 'I don't want to upset you.'

'I'm not upset,' I lie. 'You've got loads of work to do. And I've got some stuff to do for my stepdad.'

I'm out of her room before she can say anything else. She doesn't come after me.

＊

I lie face down on my own bed. When I got back to the shop this morning, a new delivery had come in and I volunteered to sort it, mainly so I could spend the day on my own, thinking and dreaming about Dan. It was too fresh, too perfect, I didn't want to talk about it and have someone burst the bubble. Maybe

I shouldn't have told Freya. But I had to tell someone. I can't believe she thinks this is about Anthony.

I met him when I first moved to London. I went into a newsagent's on Shaftesbury Avenue and he was in there, buying a magazine. He smiled at me. His eyes were really bright blue, the type that look a bit otherworldly. I blushed. We both left the shop at the same time but in different directions. I looked back over my shoulder to take one last look at him and he was looking back at me. It was thrilling. Like something from a film. I kept walking, but he came after me. Tapped me on the shoulder, said, 'Excuse me' and asked for my number. By the time I got off the Tube, he'd already texted asking me out for a drink. We went out for three months and I was happy. I hadn't had a boyfriend before. I was new in London, living in this amazing house with wonderful people and I thought I might be falling in love.

And then he suddenly stopped answering his mobile. At all – not just to me – I got other people to try. And then, after a couple of weeks, I went round to his flat and he'd moved out. I never heard anything from him again. As if he'd just disappeared. As if he was dead.

It was horrible. But it's got nothing to do with the dream. And nothing to do with Dan.

CHAPTER SIX

After dinner, I open the laptop to work on the bookkeeping I do for my stepdad, Tom, but after a few minutes, I close the program and Google 'dreams actually coming true' instead. I find lots of stuff about premonitions – apparently many people believe this is possible – but most of the sites seem a bit woo-woo and I only read a bit from each before I move on.

I have Googled this before. I think the first time was after I had the Dan Dream – I mean, the park dream – for the second (or maybe third) time, but my focus was more on recurring dreams than actual... clairvoyance. Because that's not a thing. Is it? The internet suggests it is.

But then a few pages in, I find a psychology site that actually seems legit and an article which states that dreams don't come true, they're true in the first place; that dreams just tell you what you really know – or feel – about something, but haven't consciously recognised. Which must be bollocks because how could I have known Dan when I was fifteen?

For a while after I first had the dream about Dan – it wasn't about Dan then, I remind myself, I used to just think of him as *Him* – I kept a dream diary. But I have a lot of dreams and the more I wrote them down, the more would come back to me. Before long I was spending at least half an hour each morning transcribing them and I just couldn't spare the time. And most of them were gibberish anyway. There were a couple that I felt were a bit insightful, but at the same time blindingly obvious. I had an interview for a job I really wanted but didn't get and that night I dreamt I was standing on a train platform. Just as I went to get on, the doors closed, but then the train pulled forward slightly and the next door opened. Duh.

I always thought dreams were really just your brain trying to make sense of your day. Like tidying everything up and working out how to file it away. That's why the explanation for how your life flashes before your eyes before you die makes so much sense to me. If your brain is a sort of super complex hard drive then dreams are like defragging, maybe?

I'm half reading 'Twenty Creepy Stories of Prophetic Dreams That Came True' on my phone and half watching *Notting Hill* on my laptop when my door opens and Henry bursts in, his face pink and his hair on end. He's wearing tracksuit bottoms and a hoodie, his home uniform.

'What's the matter?'

'I just walked in on a naked woman in the bathroom,' he says, his voice cracking. He shuts the door behind him, as if he's afraid she's going to follow him into my room.

I push the laptop off my lap. 'No way. Who?'

'I don't know!' He sits at the foot of my bed and runs both hands back through his hair.

'What does she look like?'

'Small? Very thin. Short dark hair? I didn't get a good look, to be honest. I legged it.'

I grin at him. 'So Freya's been on Tinder again.'

'God,' Henry says, staring up at my ceiling. 'I'm going to have to talk to her. It was bad enough when she was the one walking round in her pants, but now it's total strangers? Naked total strangers?!'

'You know she won't care,' I tell him.

'I know. She says I'm repressed.'

'Maybe that's the answer.' I shuffle up the bed. 'Maybe you start walking around with no pants, see how she likes it.' My face goes hot and I think Henry goes even pinker, but then he laughs.

'God. Can you imagine?'

'We could make it a nudist house.'

I'm not certain, but I think his eyes flicker down to my chest and it's only then that I realise I'm wearing a thin white T-shirt and no bra.

'What are you watching?' he says.

I have to take a second 'cos I feel like my breath is caught just behind my breastbone, but once I can breathe, I tell him.

'Is it good?' he says.

'You haven't seen it?'

He shakes his head. 'I've seen *Four Weddings*, but not that one.'

'Oh you have to watch it!' I tell him. 'What are you doing now?'

'Avoiding naked women mostly.'

'Stay and watch it then. I'll start it again.'

'You sure? How much have you watched?'

I'm an hour in, but I tell him only twenty minutes. I skip the DVD back to the start and reach under my bed for the tatty old cardigan I sometimes wear when I'm reading at night. It's only got one button left on it, but if I fasten it, at least my boobs'll be covered.

Henry shuffles up the bed so he's sitting next to me and I start the film again and we watch Julia Roberts dazzle as Anna Scott and then Hugh Grant weaving his way through Portobello Market.

'We should go there,' Henry says.

'We should,' I agree. We hardly ever go anywhere. We've got pretty much everything we need exactly where we are.

CHAPTER SEVEN

I'm in the park. The sun's hot on the back of my neck. My hairline prickles with sweat. I can see him – Dan – on the bench. I breathe in as I start to walk towards him. He doesn't look at me, but I know that he'll be happy when he sees me; joy is bubbling up inside me. I call out to him and he turns and smiles. I think. I can't quite see his face because the sun's in my eyes.

I'm walking, but I'm not getting any closer. But I'm not worried. I know he'll be there waiting for me whenever I get there. And then I wake up.

✻

I'm re-alphabetising the cookery section when I hear a *ping* from my phone behind the counter and I can't get across the shop quickly enough.

'You're not meant to leave your phone on the till,' Henry calls from the stockroom. It's been super quiet so far this morning, so we've just been listening to the radio – we like to start the day competing over *PopMaster* on Radio 2 – and tidying up.

'I know,' I call as I grab my mobile. I'd tucked it behind the pen holder so it wasn't out on display or anything. Henry's paranoid since one of the Saturday staff had her phone nicked by a customer and officially we're not supposed to have our phones with us at all – they're meant to be switched off and in our bags or coats in the pathetic excuse for a staff room, but no one takes any notice of that particular rule.

'Shit,' I say when I see I've got a text from a number I don't recognise. And then I notice the time is 11.11 a.m. Freya told me about a girlfriend who used to make a wish at 11.11 and even though Freya thought it was hilarious, I've done it ever since. I close my eyes and whisper 'Please let it be him' under my breath before swiping the text open.

Hey. This is Dan. From the park. Hope u remember. Want to get a coffee?

Ken Bruce is playing 'Get Lucky' and I close my eyes and dance a bit. He actually texted. I knew he would – he had to, because of the dream – but he really, really did. When I open my eyes again, a customer is standing in front of me and I shriek. 'Sorry!'

The customer – a young woman wearing a blue crocheted beanie – grins at me. 'That's OK.'

'I just got some good news...' I say, gesturing vaguely at my phone, before shoving it back behind the pens. 'Can I help?'

'I'm looking for a book for my nephew,' she says. 'He's seven.'

I take her over to the kids' section and show her a few books and only after she's bought a Roald Dahl gift set and left do I take my phone back out again.

Hi, I type. And then I stare at the screen.

'Tea?' Henry calls out from the stockroom.

'Please.'

I'm still staring at my phone when Henry brings my tea. I've typed and deleted a selection of responses, all of them rubbish or embarrassing or both.

'What's up?'

I glance at him and back down at my screen. 'I, um, met someone. Yesterday.'

'Yeah?'

I put my phone on the counter. The text box says *Of course...* but that's all.

'You know my dream?' I say, pulling the stand with the gift cards towards me and taking out a handful so I can sort them into matching pictures. 'The, um, recurring one?'

'The guy in the park,' Henry says. 'I am familiar, yes.'

I nod. I remember the first time I told Henry about it. I hadn't been working or living with him for long, but we were talking about dreams and it just came out. And he had said, 'You can't possibly believe you're really going to meet him?'

'I met him,' I say now. 'Yesterday.'

I carry on staring at the cards, even though they actually didn't need sorting at all. I'm not sure anyone's even bought one since the last time I sorted them.

'Where?' Henry says.

I put the card holder back. I can't even fake tidying it any longer. I flick the till open to check if we need a new receipt roll but that's fine too. Bugger.

'Yesterday. In the park. When I went out for milk.'

'Right,' Henry says. 'OK. And… how did you know it was him?'

'Because I just knew. I've been having that dream for ten years. I saw him there and… of course I knew it was him.'

'And you talked to him?'

I pick up my tea and blow over the surface, watching it ripple. 'Yes. And I asked him if he wanted to get coffee sometime. And he just texted me.'

'Wow,' Henry says.

I glance at him. He's got a little frown line between his eyebrows that he gets when he's confused.

'I know. But now I don't know how to reply.' I gesture at my phone.

'Well what did he say?'

'Hey-this-is-Dan-from-the-park-hope-you-remember-want-to-get-a-coffee,' I say without even looking.

'Right,' Henry says. 'So how about, "Of course I remember you. I'm free after five today. You?"'

'Yeah, that's what I was thinking. But isn't that a bit… I mean, should I let him know that I'm free today? Don't I want him to think that I'm, you know, busy and important and in demand?'

'Lie?' Henry says, smiling slyly. 'I don't know. I'm not sure I buy into all that playing games stuff. If you like him and you want to go out with him, why not just tell him that?'

'Because it might scare him away.'

'And if it does scare him away then he's not the right guy for you anyway, right?'

'Maybe,' I say, sliding my phone towards me with one finger. 'I just… I know we're going to be together, we're meant to be together. So I don't want to do anything to jeopardise that.'

'Or,' Henry says. 'If you are meant to be together, there's nothing you can do that will jeopardise it, so you might as well be yourself.'

'Ugh,' I mutter. 'That's the last thing I want to be.'

Shaking his head, Henry picks up a box of books from the new delivery and starts sorting through them, separating out the different genres and holding up the occasional romance he knows I'll want to read.

I type in exactly what Henry suggested, but I still don't send it. Instead, I stare at it until my eyes water.

'So you really think he's your dream man then?' Henry says a few minutes later, without looking up.

'Literally,' I say. 'Yes.'

'But I mean… just because you dreamt about him, doesn't mean he's right for you, does it? Maybe he's a Tory. Or he goes dogfighting at the weekend. Or he's a member of a water sports forum.'

I start to ask what's wrong with water sports – I'm picturing myself on the back of Dan's jet ski, zipping across the ocean –

but then I realise and I blush. I glance at Henry and notice he's blushing too. Serves him right.

'Maybe,' I say. 'But I need to know. And I don't know why I would have had the dream if I wasn't at least supposed to get to know him.'

'You know what I dreamt last night?' Henry says. 'I dreamt I was in the bath and it fell through to the living room and when the plumber came out to fix it, it was Piers Morgan. Sometimes dreams are just dreams.'

I frown. 'I think that one means you're feeling insecure. And the Piers Morgan bit means you have issues with authority. Probably something unresolved with your father.'

❊

I tell myself I won't send the text until I've served at least five customers, but when it gets to noon and I've still only served two – and one of those was looking for directions to the Tube – I give in and hit send. And then I have to sit down for five minutes, taking deep breaths.

I leave my phone behind while I walk up to the Indian deli on the corner and get two battered aubergine slices for my lunch and then keep walking up to the park. Force of habit. I sit on the bench where I met Dan and eat the first of the aubergine slices, the oil running down my hands, the spices making my tongue tingle. I save the other one for Henry. He always pretends they're disgusting, but snarfs one every time I buy them.

Henry gave me my first interview when I moved down to London. The manager, Julia, was supposed to do it, but she'd got held up on the Tube somewhere and, after keeping me waiting for forty-five minutes, phoned and told Henry to do it. He'd never interviewed anyone before and I think he was almost as nervous as me. He blushed the entire time and fiddled with one of his shirt buttons so much that it came off. He gave me the job there and then (to spite Julia, he told me once we knew each other better) and then, after I'd worked here a few weeks, he offered me a room in the shared house he lived in.

I'd been living in a bedsit in Acton and I hated it. The landlord there basically wanted the money from renting out a room without ever having to accept that he had a stranger living in his house. So I could cook in his kitchen, but only between 6.30 p.m. and 7.15 p.m. (and I couldn't leave any dishes so that included washing-up time too). I sometimes didn't get home until almost seven and by the time Henry took pity on me, I'd had Marmite on toast for dinner five nights running.

Henry's house was so much nicer – SO much nicer – that I almost cried when he showed me around. Not only was it just a few minutes' walk from the shop, there were no scary rules about when you could cook (or what you could cook – my old landlord had a fish ban). The only available room was pretty small – there was, is, only just room for my queen bed, a small wardrobe and a chest of drawers; I can't even have a bedside table 'cos the door would hit it – but I accepted it immediately. Henry borrowed a car, drove with me down to Acton and moved me out before my old landlord was even home from work.

✳

When I get back to work, Dan's replied.

Do you know the coffee shop by the station? How about there at 5.15?

CHAPTER EIGHT

By five, I'm so nervous I think I might throw up. The shop's been quiet so I haven't had enough distractions and my imagination's been working overtime. Henry and I have been taking it in turns to faff with stuff in the shop or sit and read behind the counter. I started reading a new US romance, with a beefy, long-haired man on the cover, nipples straining the silk of his shirt, but I couldn't concentrate and ended up listlessly flicking through one of the glossy 'anatomy' books.

I've reached the point where I think I'd be relieved if Dan cancelled – or if something happened that meant I didn't have to go: a small but not serious injury or an easily contained but inconvenient fire, maybe – so I need to get out of here and over to the coffee shop before I bottle it altogether. I just keep telling myself I don't need to be nervous, because this is meant to be. I dreamt him. I literally dreamt him. It helps. But not as much as you'd think.

'Do you need to go home and get changed or anything?' Henry asks me. He's so bored that he's starting taking shelves-full of books down and wiping over the bookcases. He keeps finding crisp packets and tissues lazy customers have shoved down the back of the books.

'I… no. I mean, I wasn't going to.' I look down at myself. I'm wearing my favourite black skirt and top with pink Converse. 'Do you think I should?'

'No,' he says, without looking at me. 'You look great. I just thought you might want to. I know what girls are like.'

I laugh. 'Do you?'

The tops of his ears turn as pink as my shoes.

'I might go and fix my make-up,' I say. 'Will you be OK on your own?'

'I think I'll probably manage.'

The lighting in the tiny bathroom makes me look wan. And my eyes look wide and scared. I add another layer of eyeliner, fill my eyebrows in a bit more and reapply my lipstick. And then I run my wrists under the cold tap as I stare at myself in the mirror.

'You can do this,' I mouth at my reflection.

And then I dry my hands and go.

✻

The coffee shop Dan suggested has a deli in the front, and seating in the back, down two steps. As soon as I open the door, the smell of pastry and garlic and coffee hits me and I almost feel my body sigh. I'm glad he chose this place to meet. I've grabbed a takeaway coffee in here sometimes when I've been getting the Tube, but I've never sat in. I order a latte from the disinterested-looking woman on the counter and take it through to the back. While the front of the shop is bright and light, the back is moodier. There are no windows and the walls are bright with neon signs. There's a white one that says 'Dream' in script, so I sit under it, smiling to myself. It's a sign. Literally.

There are only four tables down here and only one of them is occupied, by a woman reading a book and wearing headphones. I hope she leaves before Dan arrives, but at least she's wearing headphones and won't be listening to us. Or live-tweeting our first date conversation.

I check my phone. It's ten past. Even though the shop closes at five, there's always a bit of admin stuff to do after. Henry had started cashing up when I got back from redoing my make-up and I half-heartedly swept the floor before he told me to just go 'cos I was making him nervous.

I scroll Twitter, while glancing up towards the door every few tweets, and it's only just after five-fifteen when Dan appears. Because he's standing in the doorway and the light's behind him, I can't see him properly at first, just the light shining around him like a halo. My shoulders relax – I realise I genuinely wasn't sure he'd turn up – and then the butterflies burst in my stomach again. This is it. He's here. This is the beginning of the rest of my life.

*

'The interviewer was a bit of a knob, if I'm honest,' he says, leaning back in his seat. 'I don't think he really knew what he was talking about. So he was asking me, like, stuff that I couldn't possibly know, you know? And then when I tried to twist the question – you know that's what they tell you to do? Like a politician? – he didn't seem to like that either. So I don't think I got it, no.'

'I'm sorry,' I say.

He shrugs. 'It wasn't perfect, anyway. Good interview practice mainly.'

I've almost finished my latte, but Dan hasn't even taken a sip of his cappuccino yet because he's been telling me about his interview. I still haven't managed to work out exactly what the job was – or what he does or wants to do – but he looks even hotter than he did yesterday. When he came in, he was wearing a black beanie, which he pulled off to reveal such soft-looking hair it was all I could do not to reach out and stroke it back from his face. He's wearing different glasses today, rounder than yesterday's, and they suit him. They make him look sort of European. Or like a hot young lawyer forced to work on a case with the female colleague he has a secret crush on. Or something. It's possible I read too many romance novels.

'What is it you do?' I ask.

'Accountancy,' he says, nodding.

I'm not sure I've read any romance novels featuring accountants.

'Oh, interesting,' I lie.

'I'm still a trainee, basically. I've got more exams to pass. Well, there's always more exams to pass.' He laughs and I laugh too, even though it wasn't funny.

'What made you want to do that?'

He looks confused for a second, his mouth turning down at the corners. 'My dad… he works in a factory. And he loves it. He's got really good mates and he's always worked there, you know? Right from school. And I just… I didn't want that. I wanted something where I could make decent money. I thought about law, but… I don't think I'm clever enough.'

My cheeks heat up, but he's not to know I've just been having a lawyer fantasy.

'Do you enjoy it?' I ask.

'It's good, yeah,' he says, his eyes brightening. 'It sounds weird to say it's fun, but it kind of is, sometimes. You know if there's, like, some money missing and you search for it and then you find it.'

I smile and he laughs. 'Yeah. I know. That doesn't really sound like fun. I want to get into forensic accounting eventually, that's like investigating companies, what they've done with their money, how they might have lost or hidden some. It's dead interesting.'

'Sounds it,' I say. And it does. A bit. 'I do a bit of bookkeeping for my stepdad, Tom. The shop doesn't pay that well, so he's just helping me out really.'

'Yeah?'

'Yeah. He's lovely. And I know what you mean. It is interesting. Like if the figures are out and you go over it all again and get it to work out?'

He nods enthusiastically. 'That's my favourite thing really. I worked on this case where…'

As he tells me about a company who were meant to have sold their stock, but had actually stashed it somewhere and faked the figures – I think – I watch him. I like his face as he talks. He's animated. His eyes are bright and he's quick to smile. His eyebrows are expressive and he has long dark lashes. He's got nice lips and I watch his mouth for a bit, before switching up to his eyes again in case he thinks I'm looking at his mouth because I want him to kiss me. Which I think maybe I do. But not right now. I really don't want him thinking that accountancy chat gets me hot.

He's got a mole at the base of his throat and I can see a mark just under his jaw where I think he's cut himself shaving. He's got nice hands too – he's fiddling with his mug as he talks. His fingernails are neat and clean. And he's stopped talking.

'Wow,' I say. 'That's amazing.' I have no idea what the conclusion of the story was, but luckily 'amazing' works for good and bad outcomes.

'Right?' He drinks some of his coffee. 'I don't know how they thought they were going to get away with it.'

I nod. I try to think of an interesting story Tom's told me. Something about VAT? But nothing springs to mind. Instead, I say, 'Your parents must be proud.'

He nods eagerly. 'They really are. But they'd be proud of me for literally anything. My mum still says "well done" if I do a poo when I'm home.'

A laugh bursts out of me and he grins, pleased with himself.

'I can't believe I said that,' he says. 'Sorry.'

I shake my head. It's not as if I want to encourage poo chat, but that was funny.

'What do you do again?' he asks me, picking up his spoon and poking the chocolate sprinkles down into his coffee. 'Sorry, I know you said.'

'Bargain book shop,' I tell him. 'Bookland.'

'Ah yeah, course. Do you like it?'

I nod. 'It's good, yeah. I mean, the pay's not great, but I get to work with my friend Henry. And we can read the books when it's quiet. I used to spend loads of money on books, so it saves me a fortune.'

'I don't really read much,' he says, finally picking up his coffee and taking a sip. 'I never have time.'

'Oh, I read all the time,' I say, ignoring the flicker in my chest. 'I read walking down the street sometimes.'

He laughs and I love the way it crinkles his eyes. 'Do you really?'

'Sometimes. Not very often. Too many hazards, you know?'

'I can't even remember the last time I read a book,' he says, his forehead crinkling.

'Really?' I say, slightly too loudly, before I can stop myself.

'I think, maybe… at school. There was one we read that was OK. Was it called… *How to Kill a Mockingbird*?'

I smile. 'It's just *To Kill a Mockingbird*. I did it at school too. Did you like it?'

'It was OK. I was confused 'cos there weren't even any mockingbirds in it.'

I think he's joking. He's smiling, so I'm pretty sure he is. I laugh, just in case. (And then remember Amy Poehler's advice that if you don't think something's funny, you don't have to laugh. I need to work on that.)

There's a short silence, while I desperately try to think of something to say. I was going to ask him about books – that seemed like a natural progression from talking about the bookshop, but if he doesn't read, then I'm stumped.

'The shop's not that busy most of the time,' I say, eventually. 'We compete on *PopMaster* every morning. We've got a chart and everything.'

'What's *PopMaster*?' He takes another sip of his coffee, still looking at me over the rim. He's got great eyes.

'*PopMaster*? It's a music quiz on Radio 2 in the mornings. Have you never heard it?'

He shakes his head. 'I listen to Radio 1. I love Nick Grimshaw.'

'Yeah?' I say. 'My friend Freya likes him. But we always have Radio 2 on in the shop – head office rules.'

There's another short silence, and I wonder if I should ask him about TV, but then he notices that I've finished my coffee and says, 'Can I get you another?'

'That would be great,' I say. 'Thanks.'

He gets up to head for the counter and a tiny, paranoid part of me expects him to keep walking, right out of here and my life. But that's not going to happen, is it. Because he's literally the man of my dreams. Well… dream.

CHAPTER NINE

I'm in the park. The sun's shining, but there's a cool breeze that makes me feel relaxed and loose, like I could run around and cartwheel over the grass. I see Dan walking towards me from the other side of the park and instead of running across the grass, I walk towards him.

He smiles at me and happiness bubbles up inside me. When we reach each other, we don't speak, we just turn and sit down on the bench. He stretches his legs out in front and tips his head back. I'm holding a book in my hands. He's got a takeaway coffee in his. I look at the sun in his eyes and the shadows of leaves playing over his face and I know I'm going to kiss him.

And then I wake up.

*

For a while now, we've all been going downstairs for brunch most Sundays. The terrace underneath our flat has a barber's, a launderette, a letting agency, one shop that changes every few months – currently a sports accessories shop selling 'bush craft equipment' – and, on the corner, Mr C's. The cafe is actually called Constantinou, but we call it Mr C's, even though Mr C doesn't work there so much any more – Mrs C seems to do pretty much everything. She's behind the counter today and waves excitedly at us when we walk in.

'Good morning to you!' she calls, smiling so widely that her eyes disappear completely. She points to a long table in the window and calls out, 'One minute, OK?'

We sit down, me and Freya with our backs to the window, Adam and Celine opposite and Henry at the end. He immediately reaches for the menu, even though he always has the full English.

'I'm fucking starved,' Adam says, leaning back and rubbing his stomach.

'You're always starved,' Celine says, but affectionately. And then she leans over and rests her head on his shoulder. I look at Henry out of the corner of my eye, but he's still studying the menu.

'So happy to see you all!' Mrs C says, arriving at the end of the table. She's still shouting even though she's standing right next to us. 'Cheeky boy.' She pinches Adam's cheek and he beams at her.

'Full English for you, yes?' she says to Henry and he nods. 'And everyone?'

We all place our orders and Mrs C heads off to the kitchen, stopping to chat to various other customers on the way. I love this place. Mr and Mrs C have owned it for about forty years and have fought off various chains and developers wanting to take it over. It's no frills, with a black and white tiled floor, red and white vinyl table cloths, and wood panelling on the walls, but the food is good and Mrs C is lovely and almost always gives us something extra to take home with us.

'Not seeing the boyfriend today?' Celine asks me, putting her phone screen-down on the table.

'He's not my boyfriend,' I say instantly. 'We've only been for coffee.'

'But it went well, yeah? You like him?'

'It was good,' I say.

And it was. It wasn't exactly what I was expecting, but I think my expectations may have been unreasonable. Yes, I've been dreaming about him for years, but that doesn't mean we're going to have an instant connection, does it? It could totally be more of a slow burn thing. He was lovely and we got on well, that's the most important thing.

'Seeing him again?' Celine asks. She's already picked her phone back up and she's looking down at it as she asks me.

'I should think so,' I tell her.

'What about you, Henry?' Adam asks him. 'Any prospects? Got a woman you've been hiding away from us?'

Henry shakes his head, smiling. 'No, no secret woman.'

'You sure?' Adam says. 'There hasn't been anyone for a while, has there?'

Henry goes pink. 'Not since Caroline, no.'

'She did a real number on you, that's why,' Freya says. 'You need to get back on the horse.'

'Don't fuck a horse,' Adam says. 'I read about some guy doing that. Didn't end well. Actually it was hilarious. Google it, Cel.'

'I'm not Googling that,' Celine says, putting her phone down again.

Henry rolls his eyes. 'Thanks for your concern, but I'm fine.'

'You don't want me to fix you up with anyone?' Celine asks. 'There's a girl in my office I think you'd like—'

'Who?' Adam interrupts, reaching over for her phone.

'Mel.'

'Oh Christ, no.' Adam shakes his head at Henry. 'He can do better than Mel.'

'She's nice,' Celine says. 'She speaks Spanish.'

'Oh well then. I didn't know about the Spanish.' Adam rolls his eyes. 'That totally makes up for the smell.'

'She doesn't smell!'

'She does. She smells like burnt chocolate and Camden Market.'

Celine rolls her eyes. 'That's her perfume. Angel.'

'Oh, I love Angel,' I say. 'It doesn't suit me though.'

'It doesn't bloody suit her either,' Adam says, looking down at Celine's phone.

A few seconds pass and then Freya says, 'You're not asking about me then? Is that 'cos you're homophobic?' She puts her head on one side and does her martyr face.

'No, it's because I know that if you have something to tell, you'll tell us without anyone having to ask,' Adam says. 'I can't find that horse thing.' He passes Celine her phone.

'Oh my god,' Celine says, looking at the screen. 'Look what you've done to my search history!'

Adam grins at her and then at Freya. 'Go on then. Who's the unlucky lady?'

Freya sticks her tongue out at him. 'She's called Georgie. I met her through work. We went for coffee and it was gooooood.'

'The coffee?' Celine asks.

'The date. But also the coffee. Tiny little place in Covent Garden, behind—'

'Oh, I've been there,' Celine says. She's a coffee connoisseur. 'It is good.'

'So did she let you roast her beans?' Adam asks Freya. 'Froth her milk? Dunk your biscotti?' He drops his head back, closing his eyes, his face scrunched in concentration. 'Yeah, that's it. I'm out.'

'Thank fuck for that,' Celine says dryly.

'Of course she did,' Freya says. 'I'm irresistible.'

We all roll our eyes and Henry flicks a sugar sachet at her.

❧

Mr and Mrs C both bring our food over at the same time. Mr C is small, skinny, smiley, but with a permanently bewildered expression. He's hardly got any hair left, but what he has sticks directly out from his head in tufts. He wears small round glasses that are always slightly steamed up and says hello to each of us individually as he puts the plates down. His English isn't as good as his wife's, but he remembers all of our names and says 'Good bacon!' to Henry.

Once we all have our food, and Mrs C has delivered our drinks, Mr C turns and kisses her on the cheek and she giggles, pushing him away, before rolling her eyes at us.

'He's cheeky!'

He beams at her and they head back to the kitchen together, his hand on the small of her back, though I doubt she can feel it 'cos she's wearing a jumper and a cardigan under her apron.

'That's what I want,' I say, smiling dopily.

'An old Greek man?' Freya says, already cutting into her sausage. 'Bet there's loads in, like, Athens.'

I laugh. 'No. True love.'

'How do you know it's true love?' Celine says. 'For all we know, they might be miserable. He might beat her. She might beat him. They might not have had sex since 1956.'

'Don't say that!' I yelp, shaking black pepper over my scrambled eggs. 'You can tell just by looking at them how happy they are!'

'I don't think you can,' Freya says, holding her fork up. 'Celine's right – they seem happy, but you never know what really goes on in relationships.'

'OK,' I say, cutting into my own bacon. 'Well then I want a relationship like that one looks. I want The One and to be together forever.'

'I don't believe in The One,' Freya says, at the same time as Adam says, 'Why would you just want one?'

'Seriously?' Celine asks him, one eyebrow raised.

'Obviously you're my one, my precious,' he says, extending the 's' to make her laugh, which she does. 'I have already sowed my oats and now I don't need anyone else. But Bea hasn't sown her oats, has she?' He holds his fork out towards me.

'Nope,' I say. 'No oats sown.'

'Ahhh,' Freya says. 'Now I am on board with the Dan thing.'

'You weren't before?' Celine says without looking up from her phone. She's still poking at her breakfast with the fork in her other hand.

Freya glances at me and I frown back at her – I don't want her to mention the dream thing in front of Adam and Celine. They don't know about it and I'd like to keep it that way. I know Celine would think I was an absolute dick for believing in it. We watched *The Notebook* one night and she kept laughing at the sad bits.

'Yeah. I guess,' Freya says. 'But what I mean is, even if it doesn't work out, he's an oat. And Bea needs an oat.'

'More than one oat, I'd say,' Adam says.

'Thinnest of thin ice,' Celine says, poking him with her elbow.

'For Bea. Not for me,' he says, resting his chin on her shoulder. 'You know you're the only one for me.'

'Fuck off,' Celine says, but she tips her head so her face brushes against Adam's.

I glance at Henry and he's staring at them with an odd look on his face. I can't quite work out what it is.

'You OK?' I ask him.

He nods, shoving a forkful of black pudding in his mouth.

I look around the table at my friends – Adam squirting too much ketchup on his food, Celine checking her phone every five seconds, Henry with a bit of egg yolk drying in the corner of his mouth, and Freya trying to get Mrs C's attention so she can order another coffee and I know I'm exactly where I'm meant to be.

CHAPTER TEN

I don't really know why I never had a boyfriend before Anthony. It just never happened. I went to an all girls' school, and I do tend to use that as a reason/excuse, but other girls at my school had boyfriends. Some of them even got pregnant. But I had no idea where they were meeting these boys.

I went to a club once with a friend – not a close friend, I can't quite remember how we ended up going – and she told me I was too self-conscious, that I should relax and enjoy myself and wait for the boys to come to me. But as hard as I tried to relax, they just never came. They came for her. She left me on my own while she went off dancing and at the end of the night, when the lights came on, she was sitting in some guy's lap, her tongue so far down his throat I couldn't quite tell where he ended and she started.

A boy kissed me once at a house party, but I didn't know him and he didn't linger. It was like a drive-by groping. He ran up to me where I was standing, leaning against the wall, and grabbed my boob as he stuck his tongue directly in my mouth. He tasted like Jägermeister and smelled like Lynx. I never saw him again. No idea who he even was. Apart from an arsehole.

One of the reasons I wanted to move to London was that I thought I would be a different person here. I thought that when I got here I could somehow (miraculously) become the kind of girl boys flocked to. I knew something was going to be different because I knew London was where I was going to meet the man in my dream. I knew Anthony wasn't him, but the way we met was so romantic and at first he was so great that I actually stopped thinking about the Dream Man for a bit, and I didn't even have the dream for a few weeks. But then when Anthony… did what he did, it came back. And that's when I started going to the park.

I'd been to the park before I ever had the dream. Me, Mum and Matt had come to London not long before she met Tom. She came to visit a friend from university who she'd lost touch with and had found on Facebook. The friend was divorced too and living alone with her rescue Staffy and Mum wanted to see her and show me and Matt London.

The friend, Angela, lived in a new build flat near the library. The flat was lovely, but she complained about the neighbours constantly and she and Mum got drunk on red wine every single night. One morning when they were both hungover and didn't want to get out of bed, Matt and I went out on our own and walked down to Tesco to get bacon and bread, teabags and milk. On the way back, we stopped at the park and fed some of the bread to a couple of pigeons and a squirrel. It was a hot day and I lay on my stomach on the grass, arm outstretched with bread for the squirrel, the sun warming my back.

Matt lay down next to me and we both watched in silence as the squirrel approached, snatched the bread and darted up a tree. It was one of the happiest times I had with my brother and I used to think about it a lot. Actually, I realise now, I stopped thinking about it when I started having the dream. The park that had been 'the park by Angela's', 'the park where we fed the squirrel' became 'the park in my dream' and I didn't even notice.

It's kind of what happened with me and Matt too. We used to talk – when we were both at home at the same time we'd stay up after Mum and Tom had gone to bed and watch something stupid on TV – *South Park* or *Celebrity Juice*, something Mum would never put on – and catch up on each other's lives. But then he met Lydia and stopped coming home so much. I called him a few times and left messages, but we were never really the kind of siblings who talked on the phone much. Now we only see each other at Christmas, and it's never just the two of us – he always brings Lydia – and he doesn't really feel like my brother any more, more like a slightly awkward and formal work colleague. It's a shame really.

So when I started planning to move to London, I knew exactly where I wanted to live. I told Mum it was because I'd liked the area when we visited Angela, but it wasn't that. It was the park. And I know it sounds completely ridiculous to move somewhere because of a dream, but it was the one thing I felt like I knew, that I felt secure about, could count on. Moving to London was the scariest thing I'd ever done, have ever done, but the dream made me feel like something was waiting for me there. Here.

I couldn't find a flat here at first, which is how I ended up in the Acton place, but it's why I wanted to work in the bookshop. And that's how I met Henry and of course that's how I ended up living here. So it all worked out.

Mum was happy of course because Angela was nearby. She said she'd worry about me less if she knew there was a friend I could go to in an emergency, but not long after I moved here, Angela moved to Spain with a man she met on Twitter.

I do love it here though. The shops, the cafes, the park, the cinema. It's far enough from Central London that it has its own distinct personality, but I can still be in the West End in less than half an hour. I've never regretted coming here. My only regret was that in the three years I've been here, I hadn't met him. But now I have.

I haven't actually told anyone that the park, the dream, is why I chose to move here. Not Henry. Not even Freya. I know they'd think it was insane. And I know it is a bit mad, I know it is. But it made sense to me. And it makes even more sense to me now that I've met him. Obviously I was meant to come here. Obviously this was all meant to be.

CHAPTER ELEVEN

I'm in the park, but then I'm suddenly on the other side of the railings, crossing the road towards the coffee shop. It's the one I went to with Dan, but Dan's not with me. And the coffee shop isn't actually opposite the park. There's a huge queue. I know I need to catch the Tube and I know there's one leaving imminently, but I have to get a coffee first. And then I notice some pastries in the display case and I really want one of those too and I'm not sure if asking for a pastry will take too long or if the woman serving will just get me the pastry while my coffee's happening. I reach for my purse in my bag to see if I've got the right change – that'll be quicker – but I can't find my purse. I hold my bag open and rummage through it, but it's full of crap: books, a bottle of wine, loads of random bits of paperwork, an apple, my old yellow Converse that I spilled coffee on. I'm at the front of the queue and I can hear the Tube coming, so I give up on my coffee and run for the Tube instead: into the station, across the ticket hall, through the barriers, down the stairs, onto the platform, and I just manage to jump onto the train as the doors close behind me.

And then I wake up.

*

I get off the Tube at Westminster and walk across the bridge. I love this part of town. I love the Thames and the Houses of Parliament, the tour buses and black cabs. Even the dozens of tourists, bumping into each other and posing for photos against the balustrade, the London Eye in the background. I've been in London for a while now, but being near the river always makes me feel a bit giddy. I really live in London. Me!

I'm hyper aware that Dan could be anywhere, watching me as I walk to the spot where we arranged to meet, and it makes me self-conscious. I'm wearing comfy and flat ass-kicking boots in the hope that I won't fall over and make a tit of myself, but I've also got on my favourite skirt and coat to give me a confidence boost. Even so, I'm still absolutely bloody terrified.

I dodge a guy selling tourist tat from a folding table, and walk down the steps from the bridge to the front of County Hall and then along the South Bank. The sun is actually shining today and even though it's still a bit chilly, the bars and cafes are buzzing. There are a few stalls set up selling international food and my stomach rumbles at the smell of dim sum. I couldn't eat any breakfast – too nervous.

I look at every man I pass – and every man who passes me – in case it's Dan, and I'm struck by how none of them are as good-looking as he is. And none of them look as friendly. I'm looking forward to seeing him. And feeling sick to my stomach at the same time. Nice.

As I get closer to the London Eye, my stomach's churning so badly that I consider turning down the side of County Hall and just going home. Or at least to the nearest public loo. Henry's right, I can't really have dreamt Dan. Dreams don't really come true. I've probably made the whole thing up because I'm embarrassed about only having had one relationship. Or because I'm lonely. But then I think about not knowing. Always wondering. And I keep walking. There's a woman sitting on the low wall next to a coffee cart and as I pass her a man walks up and she stands and hugs him.

'Sorry I'm late,' he says.

'I only just got here,' she says into the side of his neck.

I want that. I want someone to look forward to seeing me. To hug me when I arrive. To know that I'm always late or early or that I never go anywhere without a book and take brown sugar in coffee, but white sugar in tea. I want that. I keep walking.

There are little knots of people pretty much everywhere I look, but I can't see Dan. I check my phone – it's one o'clock. The time we arranged to meet on the steps to the Aquarium. I stand at the bottom step, my back against the wall, and look up and down the path. By the time I spot Dan, he's almost right in front of me – I don't know how I missed him. He's wearing the same black coat, but it's open and I can see he's got an orange V-neck jumper on over a white T-shirt and faded jeans. He looks good. The jeans are tight and I can see he's got big thighs. I wonder if he runs. Or maybe he swims. Swimmers have the best bodies, Freya told me that. Although she was talking about women swimmers (she had a fling with a woman on the Australian team during the 2012 Olympics). But it's probably the same for men.

'Hey!' he says, his face breaking into a huge smile.

I smile back, even though my face feels frozen. 'Hi.'

He puts one hand on my shoulder and leans in to quickly kiss me on the lips. My breath catches in my chest.

'I didn't see you,' I say. 'Sorry.'

'I was just picking up the tickets.' He gestures behind him.

'For the Aquarium?' He didn't say that's what we were doing, but I assumed so when he suggested meeting here.

'No, for the London Eye,' he says. And then his face falls. 'Shit. You're not scared of heights or anything, are you? I didn't even think. It's just that I've never actually been on it and I've been meaning to, but I didn't want to go on my own. And someone told me it's romantic. Although it doesn't really look it right now.'

He cranes his neck to look up at it again, but I stop his flow of conversation with a hand on his arm. 'No, that's fine. Not scared. I haven't been on it either. That's perfect.'

*

Dan bought express tickets so we don't have to queue for long. This is a good thing because I'm too nervous to think of much to say. Instead we read the signs, nod at random details about the other people in the queue – a small girl with a bag shaped like a penguin, the words 'See you when you get there' tattooed on the back of a man's neck – and watch each pod glide up into the sky.

'This is so cool!' Dan says, once we're in our pod.

It really is. The pods are huge and hold twenty-five people (we read that in the queue). A few people have gone straight for the seating in the middle, but most are standing at the glass and looking out. I can't believe I haven't made time to come on it before, but you just don't really do the touristy things so much once you live here. I should actually try to do more. I look up. The sky is blue with just a few wispy clouds. It's a perfect day.

We climb higher and it's actually much slower than I was expecting it to be, so slow that I can hardly feel it moving at all. I look back at Westminster Bridge and spot the guy with the tat table. I watch him getting smaller. No, he's not getting smaller. I'm just moving higher.

'This is amazing,' Dan says, his eyes wide with excitement. 'It looks like a model village down there.'

He points and I look and see a tiny train crossing the bridge. No. Not tiny. Far away. Very far away.

'I love the Gherkin,' Dan says and I look over at that instead. It still looks big. Not as big as it should be, but still big. I put my hand on my chest. I can feel my heart racing.

'Oh wow!' Dan says, pointing down. 'How cool is that? There's a carousel. We should go on that.'

I look down. I shouldn't have looked down. I see grass. And teeny, tiny people. And water. Oh god, water. I look up and that's not actually better because above us is another pod. People inside a glass ball. On a wheel. Over water.

I can't breathe. My chest is tight and everything's dark and I can't breathe and I'm dying. I lean forward and my head bumps the glass. It makes a dull thud.

'Are you OK?' Dan says. 'Shit, no. Obviously not. Just breathe.'

That's great advice. If I could breathe, I *would* breathe. But I can't. Because of the whole 'I'm dying' thing.

'Count to three as you breathe in and three as you breathe out…'

One. Two. Oh shit. Shit, shit, shit. My hands are clammy and pressing against something cold. I touch my head to it too. Nice and cool. One… two… shit.

'Focus on your senses. What can you hear?'

Focus on my senses? Is this still Dan? Or do they have like a first aider in here. Someone who knows about these things. Someone who'll press an emergency button and get me out of here.

I try to focus on my senses, but it's hard to do when I'm actually dying. My life's not flashing before my eyes though. Maybe because it's too boring. I read that when your life flashes before your eyes, it's actually your brain desperately searching through your memories to find something that will help in the current situation. There's nothing in my life that could possibly help in this situation. My brain's probably scrolling through old episodes of *RuPaul's Drag Race* or *Grey's Anatomy*.

'What can you smell?' someone says.

Aftershave. Something that smells a bit like tobacco, maybe? And lemon? I don't know. And rubber. I can smell rubber. And… something really familiar. Like mango and vanilla? It's a Solero. Someone's eating a Solero.

'What can you taste?'

Metal. Pennies. Blood. That's adrenaline, I know. I think I did actually learn that from *Grey's Anatomy*. Good work, brain.

'Do you think you could come and sit down?' the voice says.

I grab at the glass – is it even glass? Maybe it's plastic, oh god – and my nails screech against it. I jerk backwards and immediately feel large hands on my upper arms.

'It's OK,' the voice (Dan?) says. 'You're OK. Come and sit down. You'll feel better when you're sitting down.'

Everything's still black and that's the worst part. Was it a power cut? No, it's the middle of the day, a power cut wouldn't make a difference. I don't understand why it's so dark.

'Do you think you can open your eyes a little?' the voice says. Oh.

I open one eye the tiniest bit and immediately see the Thames spread out in front of me. In front and below. Really far below. So far below. I clamp my eye shut again.

'Well done.' The hand has moved down to my hand now and is holding it, rubbing over the back of it with a thumb. I really hope it is Dan, otherwise this guy is way over-familiar.

'You're doing great. Everything's OK. Just breathe.'

I can breathe, I realise. I am breathing. Clearly I was breathing the whole time or I'd be dead by now. But it didn't feel like it. It felt like I was dying.

'What happened?' I whisper. My voice sounds croaky.

'You're having a panic attack,' the voice says. 'It's OK. You're OK.'

The voice is Dan's, I'm pretty sure. I would open my eyes and check, but I don't want to.

'Breathe,' Dan says. 'You're looking better. You've got some colour in your face now. You were white as a sheet for a bit there.'

I nod. I nod and I breathe and I open my eyes and stare down at my boots. My kick-ass boots. They must be embarrassed.

'Thank you,' I say. 'Thank you for helping.'

'We're almost back down,' he says. 'You're doing great.'

'OK,' I say. But I'm not going to look. 'OK.'

✳

My legs aren't working properly. I'm shaky and unsteady and feel like I could just collapse to the ground any second. In fact, that sounds like a plan. Lie down, curl up in the foetal position, forget any of this ever happened. Dan helps me over to a bench in front of County Hall, his arm tight around my waist.

'Are you OK?' Dan says again.

'I'm fine,' I say. 'Thanks. I'm so embarrassed.'

'You don't need to be,' Dan says. 'You had a panic attack. It could happen to anyone.'

'How did you know what to do?' I ask him, thinking of his reassuring voice, his reminders to breathe, to focus on my senses.

He shrugs. 'My sister has them sometimes.'

'Right,' I say. 'Good. No, I don't mean... not good about your sister. Good that you knew what to do. It really helped.'

'No problem. You want me to grab you a cab or...'

I glance at him and then back at the Thames. It looks so unthreatening from here – it's not even choppy, whereas when I was up there...

'I'm OK to get the Tube,' I say. 'I think.'

'No, no. You're not doing that. Unless I come with you.'

'No, you don't need to do that. It's far.'

'Nah,' he says. 'Just the Northern line, isn't it? S'fine.'

'Are you sure? I can text Henry to meet me at the station?'

'You should do that, yeah, but I'm still getting the Tube with you. No arguments.'

'OK,' I say. 'Thank you.'

I stare out at the water, mentally checking over my body for signs of stress. My heart is still racing slightly and my hands are a bit shaky, but I mostly feel fine.

'Maybe not just yet though,' I say. I text Henry, but I don't tell him about the panic attack – I know he'll only worry – I just ask him if he'll come and meet me. He replies *No problem* almost immediately.

Dan and I sit in silence for a while and I wonder if he wants to bolt. Leave the panicky weirdo here and leg it.

'It's incredible, isn't it?' Dan says, pointing at Big Ben and the Houses of Parliament. So not yet then.

I nod. 'I never really get used to it. Every time I come down here it strikes me again.'

'That was one of the first reasons I wanted to come to London,' Dan says. 'We came with the school when I was eleven. And I got obsessed with Big Ben. Whenever anyone I knew went to London, I'd ask them to bring me one back. I had a whole row of them on a shelf in my room.'

'That's so cute! And it *is* pretty gorgeous. I love the Shard,' I say, leaning forward to see if I can see it from here, but I can't.

'There's a nice restaurant up there,' Dan says, also leaning forward. 'We could… wait, no.'

'No heights,' I say, wincing. 'Apparently.'

'All future dates at ground level. Noted.'

My stomach flips a little at the prospect of 'future dates'. I haven't put him off by being completely mad. That is good to know.

After a few minutes – and much checking from Dan that I really am one hundred percent OK to walk, we get up to head to Waterloo. I stumble a bit as we step up onto Westminster Bridge and Dan grabs my elbow.

'See!' Dan says. 'You're not OK!'

'I am! I promise. Wobbly paving.' I demonstrate by waggling the paving stone with my foot.

'Right,' he says. 'Sorry.'

I look up at him. His hand is still on my arm. And it suddenly strikes me that this is him. This is the man I've been dreaming about. This is the man I was meant to meet. Maybe it doesn't matter that I made a show of myself. Maybe it doesn't matter that, so far, it hasn't worked out as smoothly as I expected it to. It's still meant to happen. Dan is still meant for me.

I turn slightly towards him and I see his gaze flicker down to my mouth and then back up so he's looking right into my eyes. I want to say 'Kiss me' like a heroine in a romance novel. Or something cheesy like 'Is it raining, I hadn't noticed' but it isn't raining. And if it was, I'm sure I'd have noticed. My boots aren't waterproof.

I'm still staring at him and he's still staring at me and he has to kiss me now, he just has to – we've been standing like this for too long for him not to. He smiles a little and then his fingers are on the side of my neck, his thumb brushing over my jaw. And I think, *this is it. This is what I've been waiting for for ten years. And it's about to happen.* A bus goes past and lets out one of those deafening gas brake sounds and Dan and I both laugh.

And then we're kissing. Or at least he's kissing me. I'm not sure I'm contributing much because I'm kind of stunned. His lips are soft and he's kissing me gently, his mouth really just grazing mine. I sigh and then his tongue slides across my bottom lip and his hand tightens on the back of my neck and we're kissing properly.

And part of me is thinking about how this looks. How romantic it must appear. We're on Westminster Bridge! The Houses of Parliament are behind us, County Hall and the London Eye are just to the side, the Thames is flowing beneath us. I wonder if tourists are taking photos. If I'll be able to find them on Instagram later. I wonder what the hashtag would be.

But Dan's still kissing me and I'm thinking about hashtags. I focus my attention back on him. His lips. His hands – the other one is on my waist, inside my coat, I don't know when that happened.

I tentatively slide my tongue alongside his and I'm surprised at how not-weird it feels. It's not amazing – my knees aren't weak and I'm not about to climb him like a tree – but it's good.

He pulls back a little and gently kisses the corner of my mouth.

'I need to get you home,' he says, smiling.

For a second, I can't think what he means – take me home with him? Come home with me? But then I remember: London Eye, panic attack, he's taking me to the Tube. Right.

CHAPTER TWELVE

The Tube is crammed and loud and we only manage to exchange a few words at each stop before all conversation is whisked away on the underground breeze. So many people got on at Leicester Square that I ended up pressed up against Dan, whose back is against the Perspex divider. I try to hold myself away from him, but every movement of the train knocks me into him. He feels just like I imagined he would feel. Solid and strong. And he smells really good. I glance up every now and then and pull the traditional 'sorry about this' face, but he just smiles back and doesn't seem fazed.

I wonder what it would be like to just relax against him, my chest against his, our hips and thighs aligned. What would it be like to press my lips to the skin just under his jaw? To lick over his bottom lip? Maybe I could. Once you've kissed, it's open season, isn't it? The first time I kissed Anthony... no, I don't want to think about that. I want to think about kissing Dan. Actually, probably better that I don't. My face starts to heat up and I push myself backwards again, one hand on the Perspex next to Dan's arm.

I hear someone grumble behind me as a backpack bashes into my bum and I call 'Sorry!' over my shoulder.

At Euston, we all burst out of the train like an overstuffed suitcase snapping its lock, and walk through to the other line.

'You really don't need to come all the way with me,' I tell Dan. 'I'm fine, honestly.' I'm not even shaking any more.

'No, I want to,' Dan says, reaching for my hand. His fingers slide between mine and he squeezes a little. My belly flutters.

The next train is quieter and we chat for a bit. Dan tells me he runs in the park near his house every morning and I tell him I've never run in my life, but I like parks for sitting. Which is when he asks me why I was in the park the morning we met. I tell him about the milk at work – he remembers me saying I'd gone out to get milk, which makes me cringe – and I say, 'It was such a beautiful morning that I thought I'd just have a little break in the park. I keep reading that nature's good for stress and everything...'

He nods. And then he smiles in a way that makes me know he's going to ask me something I don't want to answer. I wish I'd never mentioned the park.

'And what made you take a photo of me?' he says.

Oh god. I knew it. A guy sitting opposite, wearing long baggy shorts and a vest that shows his nipples, glances up at me and smirks.

'Ah. You saw that?' I ask Dan, shifting in my seat.

'Yup.' His eyes are twinkling so I don't think he's going to accuse me of being a creepy stalker, but still.

'I... I don't know how to say this so it doesn't sound creepy.'

He laughs. 'I'm OK with creepy. Let your freak flag fly.'

I wince. 'OK. Well.'

I have no idea what to tell him. I kind of want to tell him everything – I'll have to at some point and if we're meant to be then I guess that means he'll have to be OK with it. But I imagine Freya's face if I go home and tell her I told him about the dream on our second date.

'I like taking photos of people,' I say, feebly. 'Like... around London. You know when someone's just going about their day and they don't even know how cool or interesting they look? Well, you were sitting there and the way the light was shining... There were shadows from the leaves on the tree next to you and it just all looked really cool. So I took a photo. I'm sorry.'

'Can I see it?' he says.

Shit. He's got that excited look on his face. The one he had on the London Eye just before I lost my shit.

'Um.' I run my fingers over my phone in my pocket. The photo I took is nothing like the scene I just described. It's grainy and slightly blurred. There are no leaf shadows. No pretty light. It looks like what it is – a creeper shot of a hot man. Could I fake a panic attack now? Now that I know what they're like. No. I just need to think of a reason not to show him the photo. I could tell him my phone's out of charge. He wouldn't check – who would check? Or I could say it got accidentally delete—

I glance up and realise, to my enormous relief, that we're at my station. And then I realise I don't know how long the train's been stopped.

'Shit!' I say, jumping to my feet. 'This is me!'

I fling myself out through the doors and Dan follows me. On the platform, we both stand for a couple of seconds, expecting the doors to close and the Tube to leave and for us to have narrowly missed having to travel on to the next stop, but no. It just stands there. Typical.

'I thought that was going to be like *Indiana Jones*,' Dan says. 'Kinda disappointed now.'

I laugh. 'I know. Although I do feel like today's been quite dramatic enough already.'

We stand there on the platform, looking at each other. I don't want to just put him back on the Tube again, that seems weird.

'So…' I say, glancing over towards the stairs.

'I'll walk you home,' he says. 'It's not far, right?'

'No, it's only about five minutes. But it's fine. I'm fine. You don't need to walk me.'

He smiles. 'But I want to.'

OK.

✳

Henry is waiting in the ticket hall. I completely forgot I'd asked him to come and meet me. Shit.

'Hey,' I say, as I approach him. He's holding two paperbacks, so I know he's been to the book exchange bookcase while he's been waiting. I'd have done the same thing. Even though we work in a bookshop, neither of us ever misses the opportunity to grab a new book.

I see him glance at Dan and then back at me.

'Sorry,' I say. 'I totally forgot I'd asked you to meet me.'

'No problem,' Henry says. 'Are you OK?'

'Yeah, I'm fine, thanks. Oh!' I say, realising he and Dan are looking at each other. 'This is Dan. Dan this is Henry, my landlord. And work colleague. And friend.'

Dan holds his hand out and Henry looks down at it and then at me before taking it to shake.

'Good to meet you, man,' Dan says.

'Yeah,' Henry says, frowning. And then, 'You too.'

They both stand there looking at each other so I say, 'The Tubes are pretty frequent. You shouldn't have to wait too long.'

'Ah, don't worry about that,' Dan says. 'You're sure you're OK?'

'I'm good, yeah. Thank you so much for bringing me all this way.'

He smiles at me and something in his face goes soft. It's nice. 'No problem.'

He steps slightly closer to me and it's only then that I realise he's going to kiss me again. In front of Henry. That's fine, right? Friends kiss people in front of their friends, I'm sure they do. Dan grasps the front of my coat in both hands and tugs me towards him. It makes me laugh. And then his mouth is on mine, but it's a quick kiss. Not a peck, but nothing like the kiss on the bridge. No tongue. It's nice.

'Call me tomorrow?' he says.

I nod. 'Definitely.'

When I look at Henry, he's looking down at one of the books in his hand. It's *The Great Gatsby*; I recognise the cover. Pretty sure he's already read that one.

*

Neither Henry nor I talk for the first bit of the walk towards home. I feel a bit awkward and embarrassed about the kiss, and I assume he does too.

'How come he came all this way?' he asks, eventually, as we're passing the bookshop. We both pause outside to peer through the windows and make sure everything looks OK.

Once we've started walking again, I say, 'I sort of had a panic attack, so he didn't want me to get the Tube on my own.'

Henry stops and turns to look at me. 'You had a panic attack?'

'Yeah. On the London Eye. Apparently I'm not good with heights. Who knew?'

'And Dan was with you?'

'Yeah. He was actually great. His sister has them apparently, so he knew what to do. He talked to me and kept me calm. Well… as calm as I could be since I thought I was dying.'

'That's good. I'm glad he helped.'

We pass the burger place where I once spent about six hours waiting for Henry to get home from a date, because I'd left my bag containing my keys, phone and money at work. When I went back the next day to pay, the owner wouldn't accept my money.

I mention it to Henry. 'Who were you out with?'

He shakes his head. 'I don't remember.'

'You must do!' I laugh. 'It wasn't that long ago.'

He shrugs. Something seems off with him. He's not his usual self.

'I'm sorry,' I say. 'For dragging you out to meet me.'

'It's fine,' he says. 'I don't mind. Really.'

Except something tells me he absolutely does.

CHAPTER THIRTEEN

Freya's in the kitchen when we get home. She's got exercise books spread out all over the dining table, she's halfway through a bottle of wine and she's blasting Carly Rae Jepson from her laptop.

Henry goes straight upstairs, but I join Freya and put the kettle on.

'Have you got much more to do?' I ask her, gesturing at the piles of books.

'Oh,' she says, shrugging. 'Shitloads, yeah.'

She turns the volume down on 'Cut to the Feeling' while I fill the kettle.

'So,' she says, when I turn around. 'How was it?'

I catch her up on all the panic attack stuff and then say, 'And he kissed me. On Westminster Bridge.'

'Ooh!' she says, pouring herself another glass of wine. 'I wonder if anyone took a photo. Want one?'

'That's what I thought!' This is why we're friends. 'And no, ta, I'm fine with tea.'

'So how was it? The kiss?'

'It was nice.'

'Nice?' she says, disdainfully. 'Oh god. I'm sorry.'

'No!' I blow on my tea. 'Not bad nice. It was good! It was a good kiss.'

'You said it was "nice". A nice kiss is not a good kiss.'

I shake my head. 'I mean… I don't really have much to compare it to. But it was nice. Soft lips. He didn't slobber or bite me. It was—'

'Nice. I get it. Was Anthony a good kisser?'

I wince. I've spent a long time trying really hard not to think about Anthony. I don't want to think about Anthony. I reach for her wine and take a sip.

'He wasn't really into kissing,' I say. He thought it was a waste of time, I don't say.

She pulls a face. 'Of course he wasn't. OK, so did your knees go weak? With Dan?'

I frown. 'They were already a bit dodgy from the whole panic attack thing, but I don't think so, no.'

She shakes her head. 'I think a first kiss should make you melt.'

'Maybe in films. Or novels.' I'm always struck by how perfect fictional first kisses are. No one ever bumps heads or even noses. Teeth don't bash together. They're never too slobbery. It's all slow and gentle effortlessly becoming hot and desperate. It's not realistic.

My first kiss with Anthony didn't make me melt either. Oh, and now I'm thinking about him when I didn't want to be thinking about him. But we had our first kiss in Waterloo station. He was running late for his train. We'd been walking along the Embankment, and every time we stopped I wondered if he was going to kiss me. At one point we sat on a bench and looked out at the river and I considered making the first move and just kissing him, but I was worried that he didn't actually want to kiss me and that if I kissed him, he'd push me away and say, 'God no!' or something hideous. So I waited. And we got to Waterloo, looked up at the board, saw his train was leaving from somewhere down the escalators in just a couple of minutes and he sort of grabbed me by the shoulders and kissed me. It was a bit too hard – my top lip bashed against my teeth – and he stuck his tongue in pretty much immediately with no finesse, and then he said, 'I'll ring you' and practically threw himself down the escalator.

'No,' Freya says. 'In real life.'

'What?'

'First kisses. Should be good. In real life.'

I shake my head. 'You're the one always saying that I'm a romantic. That I have unrealistic expectations.'

'Right. And you are. And you do. Meeting a man that you've been having a recurring dream about is an unrealistic expectation. That a first kiss should give you butterflies – IN YOUR PANTS – is not.'

'I don't agree,' I tell her. 'I think the kissing will get better with time.' Anthony's didn't. But Dan is not Anthony.

'OK,' she says. 'So I told you about Georgie, right. The girl I met through work?'

'Not really. But Henry told me he surprised her in the bathroom.'

Freya laughs. 'Oh god, yeah. She was mortified.'

'So was he.'

She grins. 'OK, well, she came into work for an interview. I interviewed her. And she wasn't right for the job, but we got on really well in the interview and I just... felt something, you know?' She purses her lips at me. 'No. You don't know. Well, I'm telling you. We had chemistry. So when I rang to tell her she didn't get the job, I asked her out for a drink.'

'You did not.'

She waggles her eyebrows. 'I so did. And she said yes. And we went for a coffee – I told you that, right? – and then we went for a walk. And then she pulled me into a bus shelter and kissed me and I nearly fucking came there and then.'

I stare at her. 'Seriously?'

'Seriously. Like if we hadn't been near her house I wouldn't have been able to wait. When you kissed, did you feel it in your, you know…' She gestures at me, grinning. 'Lady place?'

'I can say "vagina",' I tell her. 'No. I don't think so.'

'I mean, I think you'd know if you had, so you didn't.'

'But that's OK!' I say. 'It was just a first kiss. The next one might be the… bus shelter kiss.'

'But shouldn't the first one be like that? He's the man of your dreams. You fancy him, right?'

'He's really hot.'

'That doesn't answer my question. But let's just assume you do. And he clearly fancies you. So why was the kiss such a big dull dud?'

'I didn't say it was a big dull dud!'

'You didn't have to.' She picks up her wine with both hands and drinks while staring at me over the rim of the glass.

'It's not all about that anyway,' I say, once I've drunk some of my tea. 'I think it was nice because it was easy, you know? Like it was easy to talk to him – after the whole panic attack embarrassment – there were no awkward pauses. I was worried he would be freaked out and run away, but he didn't. He was totally chill. It was just… like it was meant to be.'

'Seriously?' Freya gets up, opens the fridge door and then slams it shut, a Dairylea cheese triangle in her hand. 'I mean… that sounds promising. But did you want to rip his clothes off? Did it feel like coming home? Was it the kiss of your dreams?'

'I don't think so, no. But I don't have much to compare it to.'

'No, I know,' Freya says. 'It makes me want to hunt Anthony down and punch him in the face.'

I push my chair back. I think I'll take my tea upstairs. I used to fantasise about doing the same thing, but now I just don't want to think about him at all. I wish she wouldn't keep bringing him up.

'Don't go,' she says. 'I'm sorry. I know you don't like talking about him.'

'It's fine,' I say, picking up my tea.

'It's not. I upset you. And I'm sorry. I just think… it's something you should think about.'

'Yeah,' I tell her. 'I will. I promise.'

But I really don't want to.

CHAPTER FOURTEEN

I'm in the park. I can see Dan in the distance and I head towards him, butterflies fluttering in my stomach. The sun's shining, but there's a cool breeze and I glance up at the sky when I think I feel a couple of raindrops. It's only as I approach the bench that I see the man in the distance isn't Dan at all – it's Anthony.

I stop walking and the rain gets heavier, the wind rattling the leaves on the trees. Anthony is still coming towards me, but I'm frozen. He gets closer – he's staring at me – and then just when he's close enough that I think I'm going to have to speak to him, he just disappears. And I'm left standing in the park alone, soaking wet.

And then I wake up.

✳

My stepdad, Tom, is already there when I get to the restaurant. He's sitting over on the far side of the room in a booth, looking out of the window, and only looks up when I arrive at the end of the table. But as soon as he sees me, his face transforms into a huge smile and I smile right back. He stands up and leans on the table as I crane over to kiss him on his cheek. He smells like home.

'You look gorgeous,' he tells me, as I sit down and scooch until I'm opposite him. He comes to London once a month for work and he always takes me out to lunch. I love it. And not just for the free lunch. And because I work for him, he can write it off against tax, so we're both happy. He likes this place because it's just behind Oxford Circus, so it's handy for both of us.

I smile. 'Thank you.' He always says that. Always has.

'How are you? Any news?'

'Good,' I tell him. 'Thanks.' I pick up the menu. 'I sort of met someone.'

'Wow,' he says, smiling at me over the top of his own menu. 'Really?'

I nod, scanning down the sheet of white card. I'm starving. 'Yeah. He's really nice. We've been out a couple of times, so it's very early days, but… yeah, it's good.'

Tom puts his menu down. 'Is it Henry?'

I drop mine and it slides under the table. 'Shit!'

Tom turns his menu round to me. 'No worries. I already know what I'm having.'

I shake my head. 'No, it's not Henry. Jeez. I've told you that we're just friends. So many times!'

'I know, I know.' He shrugs. 'I just like the two of you together. I think he's good for you.'

'He's great,' I agree. 'But no. It's not Henry.'

The waitress comes and takes our drinks order – we both get a Peroni – and once she's gone, he says, 'So tell me about him then. It is a "him", right?'

I smile. 'Yes, it's a him.'

''Cos my second guess was going to be Freya.'

I grin. 'His name's Dan and he's a trainee accountant.'

Tom raises one eyebrow at me.

'I know. Shut up.'

'I know I'm your hero,' he says, brushing his forefinger over his eyebrow. 'It's very flattering…'

I laugh. He's such an idiot. 'Yes, all these years I've been looking for someone just like you and I finally found him.'

'Hey,' he says, fake-frowning. 'You could do a lot worse.'

'And my membership to hot-accountancy-dating-dot-com has finally paid for itself.'

'Bloody hell. Do you think that's a real site? Can you imagine?' He grins. 'I'm looking for someone to crunch my numbers...'

'Oh my GOD!' I cover my face with my hands.

'And spread my sheets... This could work.'

I peer at him from between my fingers. 'Please stop talking.'

The waitress arrives with our drinks – thank god – and we order our food: steak and fries for Tom and linguini with king prawns for me.

'Oh, and can we get deep fried courgette to share?' Tom says, smiling up at the waitress. 'You'll eat some, right?' he asks me.

I nod. It's more likely he'll eat them all, but I know he feels better about getting them to share.

'So,' he says, once the waitress has gone. 'His name's Dan and he's a trainee accountant. Is that all you're going to give me?'

'For now,' I say. 'Yeah.' I know that whatever I say will go straight to Mum and it's too early for her to start getting excited.

'He's nice to you?'

'Of course,' I tell him. 'I wouldn't have gone on more than one date if he wasn't nice to me.' This is not strictly true. Because Anthony wasn't very nice to me and I went out with him for months. But Tom doesn't need to know that. And I've learned from my mistakes. I hope.

'That's my girl,' Tom says, smiling.

Warmth flutters in my chest. When Mum first told me about Tom, I didn't know what to expect. I was fourteen, my dad had been gone for two years, and I'd heard Mum crying much more than I'd ever wanted to. She'd wait until after me and Matt were in bed, but the walls in the house were thin and I could always hear her, even if Matt slept through it. I knew she'd met someone before she even told me because not only did the crying stop, but she started singing around the house and just generally looked much happier and healthier.

Eventually, one night over dinner, she told me and Matt. She said she'd met someone she thought she might really like and she wanted us to meet him too. I remember me and Matt looking at each other across the table. He looked furious and tearful at the same time, but I was keen to meet him. I felt like Mum needed someone. Matt said she shouldn't have needed anyone but us.

We met for the first time in a Harvester. He didn't look at all like I expected – Dad is thin and dark and clean-shaven, I've never even seen him with stubble. Tom was bigger – both taller and more solid – with grey hair and a full beard. The first thing I thought was that he could make a good Father Christmas. He was kind and funny and clearly as into Mum as she was him. They started out sitting a couple of feet apart on the bench seat, but moved gradually closer until she was pressed up against his side. When I got up to go the buffet, I saw that his arm was curled around her waist. He made her laugh. He made me laugh. He even made Matt laugh, which was quite a challenge at the time.

On the way home in the car, Mum asked us what we thought. 'He's great,' I'd said. 'He's all right,' Matt had said. But Matt was the first to ask when we'd be seeing him again. Matt was the one to suggest he came with us when we made our traditional pre-Christmas pilgrimage to the garden centre – we always buy a new decoration and then get mince pies and hot chocolate in the cafe – and Matt ended up being best man at Mum and Tom's wedding two years later. Now I can hardly remember what our family was like before he was a part of it. Mum jokes that I love him more than I love her. I don't, of course, but I do love him a lot.

'So any other news?' he asks me.

I shake my head. 'Not really. Shop is same as always. Everything's fine at home – Adam and Celine are fighting even more than usual, but other than that… How about you? Mum OK?'

He nods and his face goes soft as it always does when he talks about Mum. They're still as much in love as they ever were and it makes me so happy. 'She's great,' he says. 'You know she's been working in that vintage store? She loves it.'

I nod. 'She keeps sending me photos of different clothes she's tried on.'

He laughs. 'Bought, more like. I think she spends more than she earns, drives me mad.'

It doesn't, of course. He loves it.

'Did she show you the ridiculous peacock coat?'

I laugh. 'No!'

'It's not actually a coat, or so she tells me. She says it's a beach cover-up type of thing? I said to her "Where are you going to wear that? The Co-op?" And then she talked me into booking a week in Spain, just so she can show it off.'

'Yeah?' I say. 'When's that then?'

'End of this month,' he says. By the time he's finished telling me about how they're flying, where they're staying, the various excursions and events they've got planned – Tom loves arranging holidays – our food has arrived.

'Do you want some of mine?' he asks me, already cutting off the end of his bloody steak, ready to drop it onto my plate.

'No,' I tell him. 'I'm good, thanks. It looks good though.'

He pops the piece he cut off in his mouth, and smiles and gives me a thumbs-up as he chews.

'Your mum misses you,' he says, once he's swallowed, and drunk some of his beer. 'Are you going to get a chance to come home soon? Maybe after we get back from Spain.' He puts his knife and fork down and beams at me, his eyes twinkling, 'Or you could come with us!'

I laugh. 'Thank you. But no. It's your holiday.'

'Your mum wouldn't mind!' he says. 'She'd love it actually. Go on.'

I shake my head. She wouldn't love it, I know she wouldn't. She loves being alone with Tom, she really doesn't want me around.

I've felt a bit left out in the past because they love each other so much and they're so self-contained that it's a little bit hard to be around. But they give me hope. I know that a perfect, safe, warm love is real because they have it. I know they do.

'If you change your mind...' he says, waving some fork-speared steak at me. 'Just give me a call.'

'You've just finished telling me all your plans!' I say.

He shrugs. 'Plans can be changed. Have you had enough beer yet to give me a bit more gossip on your young man?'

I laugh and then finish the bottle. I put it down on the table and say, 'No.'

'But he's good to you?'

'Of course.'

'And he makes your heart race?'

I twirl some linguine around my fork.

'That's always how I knew,' Tom says without waiting for me to answer. 'When I was a kid. And then with Janine. And of course with your mum, but you don't want to hear about that.'

Janine was his first wife. She left him for her driving instructor, which he now finds hilarious and loves to tell people. And he and Janine are good friends now. Tom's godfather to her kids.

'You know, with some people it all feels right, but something's missing. But if you have that palm-sweating, heart-racing feeling...' He shakes his head. 'You can't mistake it.'

I stab a king prawn and stuff it in my mouth. Heart-racing and palm-sweating is fine. I'm sure it's fine. I'm sure that's what lots of people want. But it's not what I want. I want to feel the way I felt in the dream and that wasn't heart-racing, that was warm and safe and loved and secure. Palm-sweating and heart-racing doesn't sound secure. It sounds terrifying.

'So?' he says. He's finished his beer too now and is gesturing for the waitress. 'He does, yes?'

'He does,' I lie.

*

Tom pays while I'm in the loo and we stand outside the restaurant, while he pats his pockets to make sure he's got his keys, wallet and phone.

'Do you need any money?' he asks me.

I shake my head. 'No. Thanks. I'm good.'

He pulls his wallet out of his pocket and opens it, flicking through the cash. 'Take this.'

'No,' I say. 'Honestly, I'm fine. Keep it.'

He folds a few notes and pushes them into my hand. 'Take it. If you don't need it, use it on something nice. Take your new boy out to dinner.'

I smile at him. 'Thank you.'

He smiles back. 'No problem. Love ya.'

'Love you too,' I say.

He wraps his arms round me and I press my face against his neck, inhaling his familiar scent and rubbing my nose against his stubble. He's always been a brilliant hugger – solid and soft and with just the right amount of squeezing.

'Keep in touch,' he says, letting me go and holding me at arms' length. 'And ring your mum. Oh shit! I promised I'd tell you to ring Matt. Mum thinks things aren't great with Lydia.'

'I've left messages,' I say, even though I haven't for ages.

'I told her you would've done. You're a good girl.'

So now I feel bad. 'I'll ring him,' I say.

Tom pulls me to him again and drops a kiss on my forehead. 'Later, tater.'

I laugh. He used to say that when I was younger, but hasn't for years. 'Later.'

CHAPTER FIFTEEN

I'm in the park. Dan is sitting on the bench and I walk over and sit down next to him. He smiles at me and then turns his face up to the sun. I think about kissing him, but I don't know how to tell him that's what I want. I wait and hope that he'll turn and kiss me, but he doesn't, he just sits there and when I look at him, his eyes are closed. I lean against him – his arm is warm alongside mine – and I close my eyes too.

And then I wake up.

✳

'I don't think they're a couple,' Henry whispers to me. We're both behind the counter, staring over at the customers.

'Because they're both men?' I whisper back.

'No! I just don't think they are.'

One of the men has a shaved head and a sleeve of tattoos down to his knuckles – it looks like he's got roses on his hands, but I can't make out the ink on his arms, I think it's just patterns. The other man is wearing red jeans and a blue cagoule and is humming under his breath. They came in together, but they've been on opposite sides of the shop since.

'I think they've been together for a long time and they just don't feel the need to be up in each other's business all the time,' I tell Henry.

'Either that, or they just happened to both walk in at the same time and they don't even know each other.'

Henry wanders off to change some promotional stickers in the window, but I keep watching the men. The one with the tattoos is looking at cookery books; the one in the cagoule keeps reading the backs of crime novels. I'm about to give up and check my phone – Dan's been texting me; he's got a couple of interviews today with a lot of waiting around in between, so he's been distinctly chatty – when the guy with the tattoos heads across the shop to Blue Cagoule and says, 'You done?'

I glance over at Henry to see if he's watching. It could all hinge on Blue Cagoule's response. Henry has turned round to watch too.

'Just a sec, hon,' Blue Cagoule says. 'I can't remember if I've read this one.'

He holds up the book and shaved head guy says, 'You have, babe. You read it in Italy last summer. I remember 'cos I laughed at the title.'

'Ah,' Cagoule says, smiling. 'You're right!' He puts it back on the shelf and they leave, both of them smiling over at me on the way out.

I immediately cross to the crime section to see if I can find the book he was referring to. And I do, he's put it back, but not quite level with the others. It's Peter James' *Not Dead Enough*. I show Henry and he smiles. 'I think they're definitely going to stay together.'

*

When I get back to my phone, there's a new text from Dan: *I don't like this building. It's creepy.*

I smile at my phone. *Creepy how?*

It's dark and there's old paintings on the wall and I think a mouse ran over my foot.

That does sound creepy.

Tell me something good.

I look up and around the shop. Something good. *I bought Pop Tarts today.*

I love Pop Tarts!
I've never had them before.
Maybe I can come and eat them with you.

I stare at the phone. Does he mean he wants to come over, have sex, stay the night and eat Pop Tarts with me for breakfast? Or does he mean come over and eat Pop Tarts? How do people know this stuff? I screenshot the conversation and send it to Freya with *WHAT DOES THIS MEAN?* Just as it sends, a customer comes in and straight over to the desk to ask for books on cycling. I show him what we've got – which isn't much, and he's offended to be offered *Cycling for Dummies* even when I tell him that's the name of the series, and not a commentary on my perception of his intelligence – and once he's left, I pick up my phone, expecting to see a reply from Freya. Instead, there's another text from Dan. It says *It means I'd like to eat Pop Tarts with you! What did you think it meant?* with a confused face emoji.

'Shit!' I say aloud.

'You OK?' Henry calls from the stockroom. I don't know what he's doing in there – we haven't had a delivery today – I suspect he's either reading or napping.

'Yeah. Ta. Just a text cock-up.'

He appears at the door. 'Dick pic?'

'God, no,' I say. 'I sent something to Dan that I meant to send to Freya. It's OK. Nothing too embarrassing.'

'Show me,' he says, crossing the shop. 'I'm bored.'

I'm a bit unsure at first because since the day of the London Eye and the panic attack, Henry has been a little bit cool with me. Not so much that anyone else would notice – and they haven't, I've asked both Celine and Freya – but there's definitely been something. But if he is upset with me, refusing to give him my phone isn't going to make it better, so I hand it over. He frowns as he reads, before whistling through his teeth.

'I definitely think he's thinking of post-sex Pop Tarts.'

'Oh my god! Really?'

He nods. 'He's not going to come up here, eat, like, an evening Pop Tart with you and then go home. That's basically the Pop Tart equivalent of "How do you like your eggs in the morning?"'

'No,' I say.

''Fraid so.'

'So now what do I say?' I grab the phone off him and put it face down on the counter, as if Dan can see me trying to work this out.

'Well... do you want to have breakfast with him? Euphemistically?' He reaches under the counter for the microfibre cloth and starts wiping down the desk.

'No,' I say. 'I mean... I don't think so. Not yet. We've only been out twice. It's too early for that, right?'

'OK. Then maybe make a joke of it? Tell him you'll meet him in the pub and you'll bring them with you or something. You could ask him to bring some too. Something cute.'

'God,' I say and lean forward until my head's resting on the counter. 'I hate this.'

'Dating's fun, innit?' he says. 'This is why I don't do it.'

'Is that why?' I ask him, remembering that he said he'd forgotten who he was out with the night I got locked out. There's no way he really had.

'What?'

'Is that why you don't date?'

'What? Because of Pop Tarts? No, that's not why.'

'That's not what I mean.' I watch him as he walks around the desk and starts wiping at random bookshelves. 'I mean... Well, what I guess I mean is, why don't you date? Any more?'

He sighs so hard, I actually see some dust blow across the top of the books.

'I mean… Do I need a reason? Like a dramatic reason? You want me to say someone broke my heart? Or I'm secretly in love with someone I can't have? I just… I'm not that bothered. If I meet someone, I meet someone. I'm just not interested in going looking.'

'OK,' I say, holding my hands up. 'Fair enough.'

The bell pings and two customers come in. It's the girl in the blue beanie who bought the Roald Dahl books, and she's with a boy. He's Asian and skinny with a white streak in the front of his black hair like a skunk. Or a vampire. Their hands are loosely linked together and she tugs him over towards the cookery books.

Henry joins me behind the counter and I bump him with my shoulder. I don't want him to be upset with me. Not even a little bit.

The girl picks up a book – I think, from as much of the pastel cover as I can see, that it's the one about mug cakes – and shows it to the boy. He dips his head shyly and takes it from her, flicking through it. He laughs and says something to her and she giggles and sort of presses against him, tipping her head back. He kisses her gently, and then glances over at us.

I look down at the desk and out of the corner of my eye see Henry swing round so he's got his back to the shop.

'Subtle,' I mumble.

He laughs. 'At least I'm not-so-subtly *not* looking at them. You're not-at-all-subtly *staring* at them.'

When I look up again, the boy and girl are no longer kissing. They're standing in front of the DIY section. The boy's behind her with his arms around her. She's got her head on one side, scanning the book spines.

'What do you think?' I ask Henry.

He glances over his shoulder, his brow furrowed. 'I think they'll stay together,' he says when he's turned back. 'At least for a while. They're pretty young.'

'They look like they're really in love,' I whisper. 'It's nice.'

The girl points to a book and says something and the boy barks out a loud laugh, before glancing over towards us again. I want to tell him it's OK, he should laugh and kiss as much as he wants. But that would sound weird so obviously I won't.

They browse for a bit longer, while I pretend to work, but mostly keep watching them. They're so lovely together, considerate of each other, but obviously really into each other too. I think back to what Freya said about feeling Dan's kiss in my 'lady parts'. I bet Blue Beanie Girl feels his kisses in her lady parts. I'm almost feeling them in mine and I'm just watching from the other side of a bookshop, like some sort of pervert.

When they finally make it over to the desk, they've brought the mug cakes book, a book about cleaning and one about growing herbs and vegetables in pots.

'We've just moved in together,' the girl says, when she sees me looking at the titles. And I'm glad, because I really wanted to ask.

'That's lovely. Congratulations.'

'It's a tiny place,' she says. 'But it's got, like, a roof terrace?'

'More like a balcony,' the boy says. He's got a northern accent.

She glances up at him and smiles. 'Yeah. But it's lovely. So I want to try growing stuff.'

'That's a good idea.' I put the books through the till. 'I've only ever grown cress. On a piece of kitchen towel.'

The boy does his barking laugh again. 'Yeah! I did that at school! And in a boiled egg. Like, the shell. So it looked like hair.'

'We did that too!' the girl says, and they gaze at each other.

As they leave, he drops his arm around her shoulders and presses a kiss against her temple.

'There's no hope for you,' Henry says to me.

But when I look at him, he's smiling too.

CHAPTER SIXTEEN

On the way home from work, I stop at the grocer's because I promised the others I'd make moussaka. Mrs C gave me a recipe not long after I moved in and it's my favourite thing to cook. Plus I can make a huge batch that feeds everyone for dinner and usually allows for leftovers the next day.

The grocer's is busier than it usually is at this time. There are at least ten Greek women standing in front of the counter, talking – in Greek – and I spot Mrs C in the middle, her wicker shopping basket hanging over her arm.

As I pick oranges out of a plastic crate and put them in my own basket – not a lovely wicker one, just the plastic one provided by the shop – Mrs C glances over and says, 'Ah! Sweetheart!'

I smile at her. 'How are you?'

She shuffles past the other women, touching them on their arms as she does, and appears in front of me. She reaches into the basket, takes out an orange, squeezes it and shakes her head at me.

'These oranges are better.'

I put my oranges back and take some of the oranges she recommended.

'It's busy in here today,' I say.

She nods and points at one of the younger women. 'Melina is having a dinner, so we all help her choose.'

I walk around the vegetable stand and she follows me, picking out an aubergine and putting it in my basket.

'For the moussaka,' she says, smiling at me.

'That's what I'm making!' I tell her, taking another.

'You ever make briam?' she says, cocking her head on one side like a bird. 'Like Greek… ratatouille. But no rat!' She grins.

I shake my head. 'I only ever do moussaka. I've been wondering about making battered aubergine like the ones from—'

'Oh!' she says, her eyes rolling back in her head. 'From deli? They are so good! But you can make yourself. So easy! Flour and egg and salt and pepper and fry in good oil. You have good oil?'

I nod. We have oil. I don't know if it's good, but it's oil.

'You can keep the batter. In jam jar. Make a lot of aubergine.'

'I'll try it,' I tell her. 'Thank you.'

'You take these too,' she says, putting stuffed vine leaves in my basket. 'No worry. I pay.'

'No!' I tell her. 'I can pay!'

She shakes her head and reaches up to pinch my cheek. 'A gift. For my favourite girl.'

She follows me while I get the rest of my shopping, making suggestions, commenting on my choices, adding a few things she says I must have. It's the most fun I've ever had buying groceries. We both leave at the same time and as we walk up the main street – she lives a couple of roads away from us – she says, 'I think I see you with a boy one day? Not Henry. Lovely boy. Or Adam.' Her eyes twinkle. 'Cheeky boy.'

I laugh. 'Maybe Dan? I'm sort of seeing him.'

'Sort of?' She frowns. 'Very handsome boy.'

I nod. 'Yeah. He is.'

We stop at a side road where a Tesco delivery van is pulling out. 'But not boyfriend?'

'Not yet. Maybe. I'm not sure.'

She wraps her hand around my upper arm and squeezes. 'You have to be sure. So make sure. Before my Nikos there was a boy. He liked me. When I was young, I was…' She describes the shape of an hourglass figure in the air with one hand and grins at me.

'And the boys were crazy for me. And one boy – he follow me and talk to me and buy me things and always trying to kiss me. And he is so handsome. And my Nikos... not so handsome.' She giggles. 'But when I let him kiss me... eh.' She pulls a face, her mouth turning down at the corners. 'And then when I kiss Nikos... *pyrotechnimata*. You know?' She makes the sound of an explosion and then widens her eyes and says, 'Oooh! Aaaaah!'

'Fireworks?'

The van pulls away and we cross the road.

'Yes! Fireworks! So much fireworks with Nikos. Always.'

'I knew it!' I say, before I realise that might not be the best idea.

'What did you know?'

I blush. 'I knew you were still in love.'

She smiles at me. 'Oh yes. We have hard times. Sometime no money. Sometime with babies. And the cafe.' She shrugs. 'But he is the one for me. Only.'

I nod. 'I'm glad.'

She puts her hand on my cheek again. 'You have to find your only one. Maybe handsome boy? Maybe not.'

CHAPTER SEVENTEEN

I'm in the park. It's dark. The park's never been dark in the dream before and at first I feel nervous. I look up at the streetlights shining from the other side of the railings and the nerves melt away. I'm safe here, I know I am. I look for Dan, but he's not there. There's a bang and I jump and look up at the sky: fireworks. Tiny white stars bursting all over the sky. Once they've fizzed out, I look down and then I see him, in the distance, walking towards me.

And then I wake up.

*

'Where are the others?' I ask Henry, turning in my seat to look over my shoulder out of the window.

'I've WhatsApped them,' he says, his phone on the table in front of him. 'No one's replied yet.'

We've been in Mr C's for ten minutes and we've got drinks, but there's no sign of anyone else and I am starving. Plus I didn't sleep well after waking up from the Dan Dream. Since I actually found him, the dreams have been changing much more frequently than they ever did before and it's starting to freak me out.

'Did Freya even come back last night?' Henry asks me.

I frown. 'I don't know. I didn't hear her. But I don't always hear her anyway.'

'She was going out with the naked one?'

I smile. 'Georgie. Yeah.'

'She likes her.' He fiddles with the napkins on the table.

'I think so, yeah. She seems very keen. Particularly for Freya.'

Freya's always been about keeping things casual. She likes to go out on the pull. She even likes being in a relationship, but generally when things start to get serious, she's out. I don't see it happening with Georgie. But I could be wrong.

A message pops up on Henry's phone and he swipes it open.

'Freya's not coming,' he tells me. 'She stayed the night at Georgie's. And then there are some emojis.'

'Which emojis?'

He slides his phone over towards me. Blushing face, tongue out, shocked face, water splash.

'Perv.' I pass the phone back. 'Adam and Celine were home though, right? I heard them—' I stop before I have to say what I heard.

'Actually, I was going to ask you about that,' Henry says. He's frayed one edge of the napkin and is starting on the next side.

I cringe. I think he's going to ask me in a landlord way. Like whether he should talk to them about the sex noise or just leave them be. I don't want to talk sex noises with Henry.

'The things Adam shouts sometimes…' He's gone very pink. 'Are they, like, normal things to say? You know… when you're doing… that?'

I cover my mouth with my hand so I don't laugh. 'God, Henry. I've honestly no idea. You're asking the wrong person.'

'I just always think they sound very… sports-based.'

I think back to Adam shouting 'You beauty!' last night and have to agree.

'I don't know,' I say. 'It always sounds a bit weird to me. Just the fact that we can hear them is a bit…' And now I've started the exact conversation I didn't want to have. Well done me.

'Does it bother you?' Henry asks, still pink. 'I've wondered about having a word with them. It's just…'

'Mortifying,' I say. 'I know.' I stir my teaspoon around in my mug, even though the tea's all gone. 'It doesn't really bother me.

It's just a bit weird. Particularly on the weekend when they have a morning sesh and I bump into them after. I always feel very… *I know what you've been doing!* Doesn't feel very grown-up of me.'

Henry laughs. 'No, I know. I've thought the same thing. I've been tempted to give them a round of applause before. Or just shout encouragement.' He turns the napkin again and keeps ripping.

'Adam would love that.' I grin.

'And Celine would have me killed.'

'There is that.'

We smile at each other for a few seconds and he looks at his phone again. 'Still nothing.'

'Bloody hell.' I crane my neck and spot Mrs C towards the back of the cafe. 'Should we just order?'

'I'm starving. So yes.'

I manage to catch Mrs C's eye and she waves at me before scurrying the length of the cafe and beaming at us both.

'Just you two today? No cheeky boy?' Adam. 'Sexy girl?' Freya. Mrs C frowns, which I know from experience signifies Celine ('angry girl').

'They might be coming later,' I say. 'Just us two for now.'

She looks at Henry and back at me and then clasps her hands in front of her chest. 'Ohhhhh. You are on date?'

'No!' I yelp. I can't even look at Henry. 'No, we're not. I told you!'

Her face falls. 'Oh yes. Handsome boy. So why is he not here?'

'He's gone home for the weekend,' I tell her. 'To see his family.'

Dan and I haven't been out again, but we've texted a bit. We're meant to be going out again next week.

She nods. 'That's good. That's a good boy.' She steps closer to Henry and puts one hand on his shoulder, staring intently at me. 'But this too. This is very good boy.' She takes her hand away and makes the 'explosion' gesture again. Oh my god.

✿

'Should I ask what that was about?' Henry says, once Mrs C has scurried back to the kitchen.

I'm really surprised. I expected him to act like it had never happened.

'Um.' I run my hands back through my hair, stretch my shoulders back and say, 'We had a conversation about the man she was with before Mr C—'

'There was a man before Mr C?!' Henry blurts out, then glances around the cafe, a panicked expression on his face.

I laugh. 'I know. And it was all good. They were supposed to get married. But no…' I do the firework thing.

'I don't know what that's meant to be,' Henry says. 'That was going to be my next question.'

'It's a firework! Obviously!' I do it again and add Mrs C's 'oohs' and 'ahhhs'.

'Never would've got that,' Henry says.

'I mean, it's clearly a firework. I don't know how anyone could possibly mime firework better than that.'

Henry raises both his hands in fists. Opens one after the other in quick succession while making a sort of popping sound and flicking his fingers.

I laugh so much I cry. 'OK,' I tell him. 'That was better. You are the king of fake fireworks.'

'Thank you,' he says. 'I'm very proud.'

I wipe my eyes with a napkin and say, 'Do it again.'

And he does. Even though he's embarrassed. He's so great.

✿

'Do you ever hear, like, a voiceover when you're walking?' I ask Henry, just after Mrs C's brought our breakfasts and patted Henry's cheek again.

'You want to get that seen to,' Henry says without looking up from his sausage.

'No, I mean like… sometimes if I'm, say, running for the Tube, a voice in my head says something like "Bea worried she wasn't going to make it…" Something like that.'

Henry puts his knife and fork down and stares at me. 'Seriously?'

I nod. Is that weird? 'Is that weird?'

'It's a bit weird, yeah.' The corner of his mouth is twitching.

'Oh. I've always done it. The first time I heard the audio description on a TV show it completely freaked me out 'cos it was like hearing my thoughts out loud. I remember being in my room, as a kid, playing a game and hearing "Bea knew she was going to win…"'

Henry smiles at me, a curious expression on his face. 'You know you can hear your thoughts out loud when you, you know, talk, right?'

'Yeah. But no. That's different. I have thoughts at the same time as I'm talking and they're different.'

'I don't know what you mean.'

I sit back in my seat, staring at him. 'What do you mean you don't know what I mean?!'

'I don't have thoughts at the same time I'm talking.'

'Shut up!'

Henry grins. 'I don't. I have the words that come out of my mouth and that's it. That's normal, no?'

I frown. 'OK, so as I'm talking to you, I'm also thinking. Like we started talking about this and I remembered the time I heard the audio description and also the thing when I was a kid. Plus there's a slight description of this actual conversation and stuff that's happening in the cafe. And I'm also wondering if Adam and Celine are OK and hoping Freya's having a good time. But I'm not saying any of that out loud. I'm saying this. To you. Now. Like this.'

'Yeah, OK, I get it.' He grins. 'Jesus, it must be exhausting to be you.'

'It is a bit, yeah.' I grin back at him. 'So you really don't have, you know, thoughts?'

'I have thoughts, of course. But I don't have voices in my head. People get locked up for that.'

'But what are thoughts if they're not voices? Wait, hang on. It's not "voices". It's *my* voice!'

'OK, so when you were talking then I was thinking about whether I do actually have the voices, so, yes, I have thoughts. But the thoughts were thoughts, they weren't in a voice.'

'So how do you hear them?'

He picks up a piece of toast. 'I just hear them. They're not spoken.'

'Weird.'

I eat most of my sausage and half of my egg in silence, and then I say, 'Can you picture stuff in your head?'

Henry bursts out laughing. 'I need another coffee.'

Once he's got his coffee, he announces, totally casually, 'OK. I've got one. I sometimes pretend I'm in a music video.'

I laugh. 'Seriously? That's much worse!'

'HOW is it worse than you with your constant narration and director's commentary?'

'Well… do you dance?'

'Yeah,' he says, pulling a face at me. 'I usually walk to work like this…'

He struts in his seat, rolling his shoulders, and then goes bright red.

'I have literally never seen you do that,' I say. 'But I'm going to demand it every day now.'

'No, but like if I'm on the bus and looking out of the window I imagine there's music playing and I'm being filmed for like the

lonely bit of the video. Or it happened the other day – I was
making toast in the kitchen at home and I was singing along
with something Freya was playing on her phone and it just... felt
like a music video. Like the toast would pop up on the beat...
you know?'

I stare at him. 'I really, really don't.'

He shakes his head. 'I think you're lying, but OK.'

I keep grinning at him. I wish I'd seen him dancing with his
toast.

'What's the most embarrassing thing you've never told
anyone?' Henry asks me.

I bite at the bit of loose skin next to my thumbnail. 'I tell
myself stories before I go to sleep.'

He shakes his head. 'Everyone does that!'

'No, I don't mean like stuff that's happened during the day.'
Which is what I assume other people do. 'I mean, I make up
scenarios. Like I'm working in the shop, alone, and Harry Styles
comes in. And he asks me to help him look for a book and...'

'No,' Henry says, his eyes crinkling with laughter. 'I do exactly
this. But not with Harry Styles, obviously.'

'Obviously,' I agree, although my cheeks heat with the suggestion.

'But, say...' He screws his face up while he thinks. 'Gillian
Anderson. She's in London doing a play. And she's looking for a
book to buy for the director. So it has to be perfect, right? And
she comes in the shop. I'm alone – you've gone off in a strop 'cos
someone's used the last of the milk.'

I roll my eyes.

'So she comes in and she asks me to help her find this perfect
book. So obviously, we look at the books together. And as we're
looking, we move closer and her arm brushes against mine...'

His cheeks have gone pink.

'With sexy results!' I say, delighted. 'Oh my god. All this time I thought I was the only perv.'

'God, no,' he says. 'Total perv here.' He grins. 'And there's no way you thought you were the only perv. You've got the internet.'

'Right,' I say. 'I mean, the only perv in this very specific way. And it turns out that not only is the daydreaming thing not that unusual, you've been having the very same exact fantasy!'

We both go pink at that.

'I think it's something a lot of people do,' Henry says. 'When I was a kid, I used to dream I could go into video games and be the character. Like I'd be Mario rescuing Princess Daisy or whatever. And then Buffy was very… inspiring.'

'I bet,' I say, without admitting that Xander, Spike, even Giles have appeared in more than one of my own daydreams.

'So I think we've both agreed – not that embarrassing,' Henry says. 'So you need to come up with something else.'

I shake my head. 'There just isn't anything. I haven't really done anything. All the embarrassing stuff is in my head.'

'I don't believe you,' he says. 'You must've done something wild. Even only once.'

'Nope. Nothing.'

'Never flashed anyone?'

'God!' I say. 'Of course not!'

'You could do it now,' he says.

'I'm not flashing you. Absolutely not.'

'I didn't mean me!' He's gone bright red, so I know he's telling the truth.

'Who then?'

He gestures at the cafe. There's a guy sitting at the far end, reading a newspaper. A woman with her back to us. A couple who are deep in conversation, with only eyes for each other. 'I'll close my eyes.'

I laugh. 'I'm not doing that. No way.'

And of course I'm not. I've never done anything like that. I never would do anything like that. So why do I feel so disappointed in myself?

'I'm totally mooning through the window once we leave,' Henry says.

CHAPTER EIGHTEEN

We're thinking about ordering more coffee when Celine finally arrives. Usually we don't stay this long. Even when it's the five of us. But I don't usually have this much fun. And I think Henry might be enjoying it more too. I don't want to leave. I could happily stay here chatting with him all day. Huh.

Celine drops into a seat and stares straight ahead, through the window, without speaking. She's wearing a hoodie that I recognise as Adam's, not least because it's got an egg stain down the front. She's not wearing any make-up and while she doesn't usually wear her full face on a Sunday, she draws her eyebrows on at the very least. She's also wearing her glasses, not her contacts, and the flip-flops she wears around the house instead of slippers. I've not sure I've ever seen her looking this rough inside the house, never mind outside it.

I look at Henry and he pulls a face that I think means 'How should I know?'

I say, 'Hey. Everything OK?'

She nods. Too much. 'Fine. Everything's fine. Sorry I'm late. Have you eaten? I'm starving. Oh no, wait. I'm going to be sick.'

She gets up and half-runs through the cafe to the loo.

'Hungover then,' Henry says. 'Bet Adam's still in bed.'

'I don't know. It doesn't seem like a hangover to me. Usually she would just stay in bed.'

'I've never seen Celine dressed quite like that,' Henry says.

'No,' I agree. 'That is definitely… new.'

'She's puking though,' Henry says. 'So... They were out last night, right?'

He lifts his arm and looks at the cuff of his shirt – he's wearing a blue and white striped shirt that's probably a bit more pyjama-ish than he realises. The cuff has ketchup on it and Henry sucks it into his mouth before looking at me and saying, 'What?'

'That's nice,' I say. 'And you're probably right about Celine. Either that or—'

'I have black coffee for Angry Girl,' Mrs C interrupts, putting the coffee down on the table in front of where Celine was sitting. 'She sick, yes? Tell her I know good cure.'

'She'll probably just have a fry-up,' Henry tells her. 'Best hangover cure.'

Mrs C shakes her head, waggling her finger at him and says something that actually sounds like 'pshaw' – 'You tell her I have good cure, yes?'

'Absolutely,' Henry says.

When Celine comes back she looks pale and damp and exhausted. Some tendrils of hair are stuck to the side of her face and neck. And I think there's a bit of sick in her hair, but I'm not going to tell her. She smells horrendous.

'Big night?' Henry asks her.

She shakes her head and, to my astonishment, her eyes fill with tears. I've never seen Celine cry. Not when Bowie died. Or Prince. Or George Michael. Not when we all went to the cinema to watch *Lion* and I cried so much I burst a blood vessel in my eye. Not even when her mum phoned to tell her the family cat had been run over. Celine just isn't a crier.

'Celine!' I say, leaning over to grab her arm. 'What's happened?'

She takes a shuddering breath. 'Me and Adam. Are over.'

God. I thought someone had died.

'Really?'

'You don't sound shocked,' she says. 'Why aren't you shocked?'

'You… fight a lot,' I tell her.

She shakes her head. 'I love him so much. I just can't—'

Mrs C appears again. 'You tell her?' she asks Henry.

'Sorry, no—'

She tuts and puts one hand on Celine's shoulder. 'I have good cure for this.'

Celine looks up at her, her eyes bright and hopeful.

'Patsas is Greek soup of lamb with head and insides—'

Celine jumps up, knocking her chair back and scarpers to the loos again.

'I will make,' Mrs C says, and heads back to the kitchen.

'It's tripe soup,' Henry says, turning his phone to show me. 'I Googled. It's tripe soup. Why would she think anyone would want to eat that?'

'Some people must want to eat it,' I say. 'I bet Celine isn't one of them though.'

'It sounds bloody awful. "One large lamb head,"' he reads. '"Use the whole skull."'

'It does not say that!' I reach for his phone and he hands it to me. It really does say that. God.

*

When Celine comes back she looks, unsurprisingly, even worse than before.

'So…' I ask, as she sips tentatively at her black coffee. 'What happened?'

She shakes her head. 'We want different things.'

'What…' I don't know what to ask. I look at Henry and he's no help. I wish Freya was here. She'd just ask all the full-on nosy questions and not even care.

'What do you want?' I try.

Celine groans. 'I want to do my job. And come home to someone who loves me. And have great sex. That's it.'

'That sounds… Adam doesn't want that?'

'Adam wants to move to Southend and buy a house and have babies.' She shakes her head, winces, and closes her eyes.

Southend is where Adam is from and he has enormous extended family there that he's still really close to. Celine's not really close to her family at all.

'And you don't want that?' I say. Even though it's clear that she doesn't.

'I do!' she says, wiping her face. 'I think. But not now! Not for years. I've got a fucking ten year plan.'

This is why I find Celine intimidating. I don't even have a ten day plan. Sometimes it's all I can do to plan for the next ten minutes.

'And it's in your ten year plan?' I ask. 'Marriage and babies and… Southend? With Adam?' I realise too late that I'm talking sort of carefully and gently to her, as if I'm a therapist.

'Yeah,' she says, draining her black coffee. 'Can you get more?' she asks Henry. 'I'm worried if I turn round I'll puke again.'

Henry waves at Mrs C and Celine says, 'Wait, no. Fuck. Get me a mint tea.'

'So you do want it,' I repeat. 'But not yet.'

It makes sense to me, but I'm not really sure why she's quite so upset. Maybe Adam would be willing to wait five years and Celine could bring it forward and they could meet in the middle? It doesn't seem to me like something you'd split up over. But what do I know?

'Yes,' Celine says. 'But now it's all fucked up.'

'Why is it?' I ask, as Mrs C approaches to take Henry's order.

'Because I'm motherfucking pregnant,' Celine says.

CHAPTER NINETEEN

I'm in the park and there's music playing. I can see a bandstand in the distance. That's never been there before. I look at the bench and Dan's not there, so I head for the bandstand. I'm rolling my shoulders and swinging my hips, dancing to the music as I walk. The sun's shining and the lawn is dotted with blue and white striped deckchairs. I look for Dan in case he's sitting in one of them instead, but there's no sign of him. As I get closer to the bandstand, I see Henry heading towards me. He's dance-walking too. I laugh and start running to him.

And then I wake up.

✻

Henry was in my Dan Dream. What was Henry doing in my Dan Dream? I'm sure it's just because I spent so much time with him yesterday and so he was on my mind. But still. It's odd how much the dream is changing. It's unsettling.

I check my phone and find a text from Dan from last night: *Free for dinner tonight?*

My stomach flutters and I smile at my screen. I'll reply later, in case he's still asleep. I stretch my toes to the end of the bad, feeling my back click satisfyingly. I swing my legs to one side and out of the bed, then let my head hang down. I could really just lie back down and go straight back to sleep. I check the clock to see if I've got time for even a catnap, but no. I need to get up and go to work. Balls.

I expect Henry to be in the kitchen, but it's empty, so I make myself a tea and take it up to the lounge – I might manage a five minute snooze in front of *BBC Breakfast* while my tea cools. I'm almost at the sofa when I notice someone's beaten me to it. There's a long shape under a duvet, man feet sticking out of the end.

'Henry?'

There's a long low groaning sound and I take a step back. Not Henry. Adam's eyes appear over the other end of the duvet, squinting and blinking in my general direction.

'Adam? You OK?'

He yawns widely and loudly. 'Sorry. Celine kicked me out.'

'Right,' I say. I'm not sure whether to sit on one of the other chairs or take my tea downstairs. 'Sorry for waking you. I thought you were Henry.'

'S'all right.' He pushes himself to sitting, still with his eyes mostly closed, and as he does, the duvet falls down to his waist. He's shirtless.

The thing about Adam is… he's hot. Like, stupid hot. Stupid and hot, Freya would say. I would never say that. But he is definitely hot. He runs most mornings and goes to the gym every day after work. Last year he did a triathlon and we all went along to cheer him on and the next day my legs were aching and all I'd done was stand there. So anyway, his chest is like a statue. Or Zac Efron. Pecs and a six pack and everything. And these incredibly defined shoulders. Delts? Is that delts? I think I've heard him talk about his delts before. Shit. I'm staring. Luckily he's still got his eyes closed.

He drops back down on the sofa, banging his head lightly on the arm.

'Bea, can I ask you a question?'

'Um. Yeah?' I take a gulp of my tea. Too hot.

'What do you think about me and Celine? As a couple?'

'Oh god,' I say, before I can stop myself. 'God. Sorry.' I walk around the sofa and sit on the armchair. 'Um. I'm really not the right person to ask. I don't know much about relationships.'

Adam sits up again and rubs both hands over his face. I stare at the hair around his nipples and then down into my mug.

'That's good, I think,' he says. 'You won't be bringing your own shit to it.'

No. I won't. I don't really have any shit to bring. I glance up. He's looking over at me expectantly.

'Um,' I say again. I have no idea whether he knows that I know Celine is pregnant. Actually I don't even know if he knows she's pregnant. 'What is it you're… concerned about? Specifically.'

'I love her,' he says, swinging his legs round so he's sitting on the sofa now.

I wonder if he's naked under there. I'm pretty sure he usually sleeps naked. I don't know whether I've just imagined that or if Celine's mentioned it. Not that I've been imagining Adam naked. Much.

'It's just…' Adam continues and I snap my eyes back up to his face. He's looking over at the TV, fortunately. 'She's great. I love her. Right? But we just… we fight a lot. Like all the time. You know?'

I do know.

'And sometimes it's about stupid shit and I think it's just 'cos I'm annoying and she's, like, precious about stuff – she screamed at me last night for leaving my shoes in the middle of the floor – but then it's bigger stuff too. Like what we both want… out of life. You know?'

I drink some more tea. 'I think… you're both very different.'

'Yes!' Adam says, leaning forward and slapping himself on the knee, as if I've given him a great insight rather than just telling him something everyone already knows. 'But, like, that's meant to be good, yeah? Opposites attract? And I did like that when we first met. That she's not like me. And I think she liked that too. But now it pisses her off. She doesn't want me going to the gym so much. I said I was thinking of doing an Iron Man and she looked at me like I'd shit in her pocket.'

I laugh. I can imagine that exact look.

'I think maybe you need to talk to her?' I say. That's always good relationship advice, right? You can't go wrong with talking. I hope.

'Celine's not really into talking,' Adam says, tipping his head forward and rubbing the back of his neck. 'She likes to resolve things more… physically.'

My face heats immediately.

'You can all hear us, right?' Adam asks.

I nod. I'm staring down at the floor. There's no way I can look at him now. Instead I stare at the orange stain on the carpet, made when Henry knocked a pot of mango chutney off the coffee table a couple of months ago.

'I think she gets off on it,' Adam says.

God. It is way too early for this.

'Sorry,' Adam says. 'I was just lying awake for a while, thinking, and I'm a bit…'

I don't look up, so I don't know if there's a gesture or expression to accompany whatever it is he is.

'I didn't mean to embarrass you,' he says.

'I'm not embarrassed,' I say. Even though I know full well my face is burning red.

'Can I just ask one more thing?' he says.

I nod. I think.

'Is it, like, a problem? For you and Henry and Freya? Hearing us, I mean?'

'Do you mean… um…' I manage to say.

'Both, I guess. Fighting and fu— the other thing.'

My face is now so hot it's actually starting to hurt. I picture it sizzling. Like a fajita.

'I don't think so?' I say. 'As long as it's not too late. On a weeknight.' That's truly the most pathetic answer I could possibly have given. I'm embarrassed for myself. Please keep your fighting and fucking to early evenings and weekends!

Adam laughs, at least. 'Right. OK.'

'I did say I wasn't the best person to talk to about this.'

'No,' he says. 'That's been really helpful.'

'I doubt it. I'm sorry.'

Adam grins at me and stands up. He's wearing pants, thank god. Tiny bright blue pants. I stare back at the mango stain again.

'Morning,' he says and I look up to see Henry at the door. He looks at Adam and then at me. His hair's standing on end and he's still in his pyjamas – red pyjama bottoms and a shapeless white T-shirt. Henry in pyjamas! A never-before-seen sight!

'I overslept,' he says.

'Shit!' I grab my phone. I hadn't even thought about the time. Or work. 'We'll be OK if we leave in the next fifteen minutes,' I tell Henry.

'Thanks for the talk, Bea,' Adam says. He's rolled his duvet up and is heading out of the room with it under his arm. He fist-bumps Henry on the way past and Henry's eyebrows pull together with confusion.

'He slept on the sofa,' I tell him. 'He and Celine had a row.'

'Right,' he says. He glances over his shoulder to make sure Adam's gone. 'Does he know?'

'It doesn't sound like it, no.'

'Shit.'

I drink the last of my tea and leave Henry in the lounge while I have a very quick shower. When I'm done, Henry is dressed and ready to leave, his hair still wet from the shower too.

During the five minute walk to the shop, I recap my conversation with Adam.

'I just assumed they were both cool with it,' Henry says. 'The fighting and the making up.'

I glance at him. The tips of his ears have gone pink.

'I don't understand it,' I tell him, as we wait at the traffic lights. 'I know that arguments are meant to be healthy in a relationship or whatever. But maybe not that much?'

Henry shrugs. 'Me and Caroline used to argue, even have massive rows sometimes, but nowhere near as much as Celine and Adam.'

I want to ask him about the making up afterwards, but I can't bring myself to do it. I wonder if he's thinking about it now too.

He nods. 'You never met Caroline, did you?'

'No,' I say. 'You were together for a while?'

He's talked about her before. A little. Usually when drunk.

'Four years,' he says.

'Bloody hell.'

A bus passes and then we cross.

He laughs, humourlessly. 'Yeah. We were fourteen when we first started going out together and I know no one expected us to stay together – I didn't either – but it was just so easy. We were really happy. But then we went to different universities. We'd planned to go to the same one to begin with – she was going to come to London too – but then she said she thought it would be better if we had a bit of space.'

'Oh-oh.'

'Yeah. You see, you say that. I agreed with her. I was thinking about meeting her at the station and having weekends together and how romantic it would be to do the long-distance thing. And it was, at first. I remember going to meet her at Euston and she ran up the ramp – you know, from the trains?'

I nod and steer him around a guy heading into the grocer's with a pile of fruit crates on a tip-up trolley.

'She ran up the ramp and practically jumped on me. She nearly knocked me on the floor, you know. But people were looking and she was kissing me and it was just... it's still one of my best memories.'

'So what happened?'

'She invited me up to stay with her – she was at Sheffield and she loved it. She said she wanted to show me the university and her halls and for me to meet her friends and everything. But I knew within about half an hour of being there that she'd fallen in love with someone else.'

'No!' I actually stop walking, I'm so shocked. 'But why would she invite you, if—'

'I think she was trying to convince herself to stay with me. Maybe. Or she wanted to compare us? I don't know. But I spent the weekend being a passive aggressive arsehole and then when I got home she rang me and finished it.'

'I'm sorry,' I say. 'That sucks.'

'Yep.'

We pass the cinema and Subway – I don't really know what to say – and then a laugh bursts out of him.

'The look on your face when Adam stood up in those tiny pants.'

I let out a bark of laughter of my own and immediately cover my mouth with my hand. 'Oh my god, I know! What were they?!'

'I think the Australians call them "budgie smugglers",' Henry says.

I laugh again. 'To be honest, it was kind of a relief. I thought he might be naked.'

'Fuck, don't say that. I'll have to get the sofa covers cleaned.'

CHAPTER TWENTY

'Third date?' Freya says, waggling her perfectly threaded eyebrows at me. We're in her room again, lying on the bed, propped up against the headboard. She's bought one of those lamps that looks like a film spotlight. She buys something beautiful for her room every payday. The last thing I bought for mine was a condensation trap.

'Yes.'

I still feel sick with nerves, but I'm assuming that's normal. People talk about having butterflies like it's a good thing. I would like them all to die.

Freya wolf whistles, clicks her teeth, rolls her eyes. 'Is he on a promise?'

'God,' I say. 'No.'

'Does he know that?'

'Is that really a thing?' I ask her, before drinking some more of the beer Freya insisted on for Dutch courage. 'Like people expect sex when you get to a certain date, rather than it just happening, you know, naturally?'

She reaches over and cups my cheek with her hand. 'Oh, my sweet summer child.'

'Shut up. It just makes no sense to me. Like, are we going to get the bill and then be like "Welp, guess it's time to go and have some sex now!"?'

'I mean… maybe? But it's more likely that he'll just be expecting that's how the evening will end. He'll have shaved his balls—'

I pull a face.

'And bought a multi-pack of condoms and made sure his roommates aren't home, all that.'

'God.'

'Are you, you know?' She whistles again and gestures at my crotch. 'All sorted? Down there?'

'God. I think so? I mean, I've done my bikini line.' Just the thought of Dan being anywhere near my bikini line is making my ears go hot, and not in a good way.

'Just your bikini line? You're still full bush?' Freya nods. 'Retro.'

'That's still OK, isn't it? I mean, it's not, like, down my legs or anything. It's neat.'

'Hey,' Freya says. 'You do you. I think some men expect, like, a Brazilian still. Or the full Hollywood. 'Cos they're all off their tits on porn. It's more flexible in my circles. I've gone French – landing strip. But I'm going to grow it back 'cos it's itchy as fuck.'

'I don't want that,' I say. Just the thought of it is making me want to scratch.

'S'fine. I mean, if he judges you on your pubes you don't want him anyway, right?'

I nod, remembering how I had my one and only waxing done after Anthony commented on the state of my bikini line.

'And you know you don't have to do anything if you don't want to?'

'God. Of course.'

'I mean, I know you. I don't want you to feel pressured.'

'You're the one making me feel pressured with all this third date bollocks.'

'Sorry.' She looks genuinely contrite. For once. 'I just don't want you to be surprised.'

'And you really think he'll be expecting it?'

'I think he'll be expecting things to move on a bit, yeah. At least.'

'Fuck.'
'Indeed.'

*

Following the conversation with Freya, I put a bit more effort into getting ready for our date that I have previous dates. The thought of potentially taking my clothes off in front of Dan makes me feel sick with nerves. But that's normal, right? Having sex with a new person for the first time is nerve-wracking.

My first time with Anthony was my first time with anyone and it was unsurprisingly disappointing. I'd been incredibly nervous and so had too much to drink and don't actually remember much about it except very clearly thinking 'Is this it?' I wasn't sure what all the fuss was about. Things improved over the next couple of months, but it still never actually got good. Not for me, anyway. He always seemed to enjoy it.

But whether I'm going to sleep with Dan or not tonight, a bit of preparation is definitely required. I exfoliate, shave and moisturise. I think about fake tan, but I'm rubbish at it and if we do end up having sex there's no way we'll be doing it with the lights on, so I think I can stay my usual pale self.

I wonder if I should be the one to buy condoms. Equality and everything. But then that would suggest (to who? I don't know) that I'm planning to have sex and I am definitely not planning to have sex. If we both get swept away and end up having sex then I'm sure… Yeah, I'd better buy some condoms on the way.

I put on my favourite (and only) set of matching underwear. It's not particularly sexy, but it's nice and new-ish. I think about stockings and heels and roll my eyes at myself. I've never worn stockings in my life. I don't even own any. I could nip to Tesco and buy some hold-ups, but why? I've got this image in my mind of what preparing to have sex is meant to look like and I don't exactly know where I've got it from. Films, books, TV? A combination?

The thing about the romantic comedies I love is that they often skim over the sex scenes. The older ones literally fade to black (if they get anywhere near a hint of sex in the first place) and even the more recent ones are pretty coy. Meg Ryan's fake orgasm is about as explicit as it gets and she's fully dressed in a cafe.

Romance novels are often more detailed (sometimes a lot more) but I find it hard to picture it when I'm reading and I really can't imagine myself actually doing most of it. And almost everyone in the novels I read have more experience than me.

I wear a mid-length black dress that I love. It's comfy, but also clingy so I hope it's sexy. I'm pulling on my Converse when I realise I don't know what kind of restaurant we're going to. It might be too fancy for Converse, so I yank them off and put my black loafers on instead – they've got a bright pink sole. I love them, but they hurt like hell after about half an hour so I don't wear them much. Hopefully I'll be sitting down for most of the evening. Or lying down. No. Don't think about that.

I shower my hair in salt spray, fill in my eyebrows, slick on bright pink lipstick and I'm ready to go.

I wonder if I can sneak out without anyone seeing me, but when I get downstairs, I find Freya, Adam and Celine in the kitchen. Adam and Celine are sitting at the table and Freya's standing in front of the oven. The windows are steamed up and something's bubbling on the stove; it smells of garlic and bacon. Am I missing carbonara? I love carbonara.

Freya wolf whistles at me. 'Get it, Bea.'

I shake my head, laughing. 'Oh shut up.'

'You look gorgeous,' Celine says. 'Love those shoes.'

'Yeah?' I look down at my dress and my shoes that are already slightly pinching, but it'll be fine once I'm on the Tube.

'I would,' Adam says and Celine smacks his arm. She's got her hair pulled back in a tight ponytail and she looks sweaty and wan. She still hasn't told Adam she's pregnant. She came to my room the other night and watched half of *Crazy, Stupid, Love* with me and she was so feeble that she hardly even took the piss, so I've no idea how he hasn't worked it out. Clueless.

'Don't forget what we talked about,' Freya says, raising one eyebrow at me.

'Ohhhh,' Celine says. 'Is tonight the night? Is that why you look so…?'

'So what?' I say. 'How do I look?'

'Hot,' Freya says.

Celine nods. 'That's what I meant. Sexy.'

'Oh god,' I say. 'Really?'

Is Dan going to think so too? Is he going to think it means I'm ready to have sex?

'You don't have to do it if you don't want to!' Freya says again, obviously reading my mind. Or seeing the panic on my face.

'I know,' I say. 'Don't worry. I'm twenty-five years old. I'm not going to have sex just because—' I don't get to finish the sentence because at that moment, Henry walks in and stops dead in the doorway, staring at me.

He doesn't look away and my face starts to heat up. Why isn't he looking away?

'You look…' he starts to say.

'Doesn't she look hot?!' Freya interrupts him.

He shakes his head but as if he's trying to clear it rather than because he disagrees.

'You look great,' he says, still looking at me.

I can't seem to look away either. His cheeks have gone pink and I dread to think how much I'm blushing, but I'm still just standing there, staring at him and he's just standing there, staring at me. My stomach flutters with nerves. Or—

'What time are you meeting him?' Adam says.

For a second, I can't even think who he means and then I say, 'Oh! Shit. Yeah, I've got to go.'

I don't want to go.

'I'll see you all later,' I say.

And then I leave.

CHAPTER TWENTY-ONE

It only takes me a couple of minutes to walk up to Seven Dials from Leicester Square Tube – it's a lovely evening, the sun is low in the sky and it's warm enough that I've had to take my leather jacket off but I'm already limping when I get there. I walk around the monument to make sure Dan's not sitting on the other side (it's small enough that I'm sure we'd be able to see each other, but I don't want to take any chances) and sit down between a man wearing a backpack and staring down at his phone and a woman in black leather trousers and stilettos, also staring down at her phone.

I want to take my shoes off, even just for a second, but I'm scared I won't be able to get them back on. Instead I circle my ankles and try to breathe through the pain.

I'm considering hobbling off to find somewhere to buy flip-flops when I see Dan getting out of a black cab in front of the Cambridge Theatre. He's wearing a black and white stripy top, black jeans and black shoes with a brown sole.

'Hey,' he says, as soon as he reaches me. 'Cool shoes.' He lifts his foot to show me his.

'I'm in agony,' I say without standing up. 'Can you get a takeaway and we'll have it here?'

He laughs. His face is really nice, especially when he smiles. 'We could do. But I've booked a table… I could give you a piggy back?'

I shake my head, reaching one hand out so he can pull me up. 'I'll be OK. I'll just have to stop and cry every now and then.'

Once I'm upright, he slides his arm around my waist. 'Lean on me, yeah?'

The first few steps are blinding agony, but as we head up Monmouth Street it dulls to more like blistering pain.

'I could give you a fireman's lift, maybe?' Dan says. 'I always wanted to be a fireman.'

'Yeah? Why didn't you?'

He shrugs. 'I don't know really. I never actually thought of it as a real job. It was like when I was a kid, you know? Like kids want to be a fireman or a train driver or... what is it for girls? A ballerina?'

I laugh. 'I never wanted to be a ballerina.'

'What did you want to be?' he asks as we pass Brasserie Max, which is where I'd assumed we were going when he suggested meeting at Seven Dials.

'Did you ever watch *Pop Idol*?'

'No, I don't think so.'

'It was like *X Factor* before *X Factor*. There was *Popstars* where they made a band and then another where they made rival bands and then *Pop Idol*. Will Young won it.'

'Oh yeah,' Dan says. 'I know him.'

'I can't sing so I never thought about being a pop star or anything, but they had judges – like *X Factor* – and one of them was this woman, Nicki Chapman? And I wanted to be her. I wanted to encourage the bands and advise them and maybe take them shopping, get their hair cut, singing lessons, all that.'

'You could do that, couldn't you?'

'Maybe? Like in PR. But I really don't think I'm suited to it. I wrote her a fan letter though, she was really sweet.'

Dan laughs. 'I wrote one to David Beckham.'

'Ooh! Did he reply?'

'He sent a signed photo. I had it framed on my bedside table.'

At the top of Monmouth Street we cross the road and Dan says, 'This is the place.'

It's a diner. Called The Diner. It looks nice, but not quite what I was expecting. It doesn't say 'expecting to have sex tonight' to me, which actually drains some of the tension from my shoulders.

'It looks great,' I say.

'You don't care where we go, do you? You just want to sit down.'

'I might weep tears of joy, yes.'

We're seated immediately, thank god, in a booth in the window and I prise my shoes off and stretch out my toes, groaning with relief.

'I'll never get them back on,' I say. 'But I'll walk home barefoot, I don't even care.'

Dan dips his head to look under the table and I pull my feet up.

'God, don't look! They'll be horrifying!'

'Nah,' he says. 'I bet you've got cute feet.'

I don't even know what to say to that, so I hide behind my menu instead.

We order drinks and while we wait, I pull my feet up to poke at the more painful bits while Dan tells me about the interviews he's had.

After our drinks arrive and I'm still rubbing my feet and wincing, Dan says, 'Would plasters help? I could go and get some plasters.'

'I think I'm beyond help, to be honest, but thank you for offering.'

'Or maybe socks?' He takes out his phone and starts tapping and by the time I've chosen meatloaf with a side of mac and cheese, he says, 'A-ha!'

'What?'

'There's an actual sock shop just round the corner. What size are you?'

'Five, but—'

He's already sliding along his seat. 'Order me the burrito and I'll be back in five minutes.'

'You really don't have to—'

'You're in pain. I'll be five.'

He disappears out of the door and I look back at the menu. I can't believe he's gone to buy me socks. Once, Anthony and I went out for dinner and then back to his place. I started to feel sick and he said I'd had too much wine, but then I threw up and started having excruciating stomach pains. I was lying on the bed, holding my stomach, trying not to cry, the bathroom bin next to me in case I vomited again, and Anthony told me he'd called me an Uber. He said he had work in the morning and couldn't risk not getting a good night's sleep. I had to stop the Uber three times on the way home to throw up at the side of the road.

*

The waiter has been and taken our order by the time Dan comes back with a three-pack of socks in red, yellow and blue and a two-pack in white and black ('I didn't know what colour you wanted'). I feel much better as soon as I put them on (I go for the red ones). I still can't get my shoes back on, but I'm much more hopeful than I was earlier.

'Stylish,' I say, holding out one foot and twirling my ankle.

'No!' he says. 'It actually is! I've seen stuff like that in magazines, where, like, you don't think it would work but it's ironic or something.'

'You read fashion magazines?'

'My sisters get them.'

'You've got sisters?' As I say it I realise he told me about one of them after I had the panic attack.

'Three. They still live back in Derby.'

'Ah, Derby. I was wondering where your accent was from.'

'Yeah. What about you?'

'Just outside Manchester. My parents still live there.'

'Yeah, all my family's still in Derby. Just me down here.'

'How come you moved down here?'

'For the original traineeship. I'm not planning to stay here long-term.'

'No?'

'Nah, I want to go where the money is. Dubai, maybe. A guy I was at uni with works somewhere out there and he is coining it in.'

'I've never really fancied it,' I say. 'Too new and shiny. I love the history in London.'

'History's boring,' Dan says.

I don't mean to react, but he obviously sees something in my expression 'cos he says, 'I mean, I know it's all really interesting and everything if you're into it – my mum is, she reads, like Dickens and stuff about kings and queens – but I've just never really been interested.'

'I remember when I was a kid,' I tell him. 'My mum was always pointing stuff out to me. Like, we went to York and she was fascinated. I remember her touching a wall and saying it was the same wall that Romans had touched and I was like "yeah, whatever, big deal". But that'd be me now. I love it.'

The waiter brings our food and once he's gone, Dan says, 'It's more interesting when you put it like that. Like, if someone can bring it to life for you? But at school it was all just dates and laws and shit I couldn't remember and couldn't get straight in my head. Is that why you wanted to move to London? The history?'

I shake my head. 'That's part of it, I think? But really it's just because London feels like the centre of everything. From the very first time I came, I knew I wanted to live here. I used to have postcards all over my wall. And we came every year for my birthday. I didn't get presents for years; I'd have a day in London.'

'What do you love about it?'

I frown and take a sip of my Red Slushy cocktail, which I chose because it looked and sounded like an actual slushy, but which I am now worrying is staining my mouth red… like an actual slushy.

'I'm not sure exactly. The energy, I guess? I feel like it's full of possibilities. Like at home I would have to be a certain thing, but here I can do or be anything.'

'And what do you want to be?'

'Ah. That's a different issue.'

'You don't know?'

'Not really. I've thought about my own bookshop. Like a bookshop/coffee shop, maybe? But I'd need a lot of money for that and… I have no money. Right now I'm happy working in the bookshop. It's fun working with Henry and there's no responsibility… It's not ideal long-term, I know.'

'But you're only young.'

'Yeah,' I say. 'That's what I keep telling myself. What do your sisters do?'

'Katie is a teaching assistant at my mum's school – Mum's a teacher – and Tanya and Beth both work at a spa place doing, like, massage and treatments.'

'That sounds cool.'

'Yeah. They love it. They were always into beauty stuff. They used to give me facials when I was at home.'

I grin. 'Yeah?'

'And once I let them wax my legs. And my chest.'

I think of my bikini line and wonder again if it would be horrifying to Dan like it was to Anthony. I can't imagine Henry caring about something like that. And I don't know why I'm thinking about Henry right now. I drink some more of my drunken slushy and Dan says, 'Do you have to get back?'

'No. What were you thinking?'

'Well, I was going to suggest a romantic walk along the Thames, but…' He grins. 'There's a nice bar just over the road. It's usually packed inside, but there's a sort of beer garden that's nice, if you're OK with people smoking?'

'That sounds good,' I say.

Dan pays – I offer, but he insists, even though I tell him I already owe him for the socks – and then we leave. The bar is literally just over the road and down a side street and the beer garden is cute: small and square with only four picnic tables, and people smoking at just one of them. I sit down and Dan goes inside for drinks. I text Freya.

Tonight might be the night

Almost immediately she replies with a heart, an aubergine and a rocket emojis. Immediately followed by *You sure?*

'No,' I say aloud. And then tap it into my phone.

Don't do it unless you're sure. Promise.

One hundred per cent? I don't know if I've ever been one hundred per cent sure of anything in my entire life.

Seventy-five should do it, she replies. *Did you get condoms?*

I send back the thumbs up emoji. I got them in Tesco on the way to the Tube. I felt weird taking them up to the counter – I couldn't take them on their own, I also bought a *Guardian* and a packet of Revels – sort of shifty but also grown-up. Like I had a flashing sign over my head saying 'May be getting laid'. The woman serving didn't even blink. And I'm not sure I'm mature enough to be having sex if I get overexcited just buying the condoms.

Dan comes back with the drinks and for a minute or so we sit in silence.

'Do you—' he says.

'What's the—' I say at the same time.

'You go,' he says.

'I was just going to ask if you ever hear like a running commentary in your head? I was talking to my flatmate about it – Henry? You met him at the station? – the other day and I was just thinking about it.'

He looks confused. 'Like a voice in my head?'

'Yes! Like a voice telling you what's happening?'

He shakes his head. 'Never. No.'

'Really? Like when you were in the bar, there was a voice in my head saying, like, "Dan's gone to the bar" and…' I realise I can't tell him the other stuff I was thinking. 'And, you know, just, like, observations.'

He laughs. 'No. That sounds mental.'

I drink some of my beer. 'What were you going to say?'

'Oh!' he says. 'I was just going to ask if you go home a lot. But that sounds really boring now.' He smiles behind his glass.

'No,' I say. 'It doesn't. I don't get home that much, no. Just special occasions really. The train's quite expensive and… I don't know, it just doesn't happen. I used to go home whenever my brother came home but he hardly does any more. What about you?'

He nods. 'I try to get home as much as I can, yeah.'

A pigeon flies into the beer garden and we both watch it wandering between the tables for a bit. I'm struggling to think of something to say and the more I struggle, the more stressed I get. Eventually I say, 'The other thing me and Henry were talking about the other day was the most embarrassing thing you've ever done that no one knows.'

'God,' he says, covering his mouth with his hand. 'Too many to choose from.' He drops his head back, looking up at the sky, and then says, 'When I was at school I liked this girl. Portia. I wrote a note asking her out and my mate passed it to her. She sent it back saying yes. I was leaning back on my chair. On two legs, you know? Like the teachers always tell you not to. And when I read her note, I just fell right back. Flat on the floor.'

'Oh no!' I say, laughing. 'That's pretty bad. Although we actually had a teacher do that once, it was great. But that doesn't count, people know about that one. Portia. And whoever else was in the class.'

'Oh, you're right,' he says. 'Forgot that bit.' He thinks a bit longer and then says, 'OK. No one knows this one. At one of my job interviews I went to the loo and then couldn't get back to the interview room. There was a keypad on the door and I didn't know the code. Ended up climbing out of the window.'

'You did not.'

He nods. ''Fraid so. What about you? What's your most embarrassing moment?'

'That panic attack on the London Eye was pretty shameful.'

'Nah. You're going to have to come up with something better than that.' He smiles.

'OK…' I try to think. Most of my embarrassing moments are too embarrassing to share with someone I might potentially be thinking about sleeping with. 'I went to Alton Towers with some friends and my boob came out of my top on one of the rides. I didn't realise – I could just see all these blokes going "Waaaaahey" every time I went past. It was only when it got to the end that I looked down and saw. I was terrified someone had filmed it and it would go viral.'

'Which one?' he asks, grinning.

I look down at my chest and point at my left boob. 'This one.'

He laughs. 'Which ride?'

'Oh god. OK, so I can add that to the list.' I shake my head. 'The Runaway Mine Train.'

His eyes flicker down to my chest. 'You probably looked amazing.'

'I doubt it very much. But thanks.'

He swigs some of his drink, a line of foam settling on his top lip. I want to reach out and wipe it away with my thumb, but it seems like too much. He wipes it with the back of his hand and then shuffles along his seat and moves round the table to sit next to me.

'Hi,' he says, his voice lower.

'Hi.' I have to look up at him a little with him this close. I think I like it.

He runs his thumb along the back of my forearm and then circles my wrist with his hand.

My heart's racing and I worry he'll be able to feel my pulse under his thumb. Maybe that's what he's doing – he thinks I'm so dull, he was worried I might be dead and he's come round to check. But no, I was just talking about my boobs – well, actually Freya's boobs because that was her story, not mine. My embarrassing stories aren't flirty enough, so I decided to nick one of Freya's because all of hers are—

And he's kissing me.

Sometimes in the romance novels I read, the heroines are freaking out and the heroes kiss them and all the thoughts go out of their head and all they can think about is the kiss. That doesn't seem to be the case for me. Even though I do think this is a better kiss than the one on the bridge.

I need to focus on the kiss. His lips. Moving against mine. Slowly. They're soft and not too wet and his thumb is stroking the back of my hand and it feels nice. I don't know where his other hand is and I don't know where mine is either. Where is it? Oh, it's on my thigh. OK. I should move it.

I curl my fingers into his T-shirt. He shuffles even closer. I could press up against him if I wanted to, but I'm aware that there are other people here, even though I've got my back to them and I can hear them talking and laughing so I know they're not sitting staring at us and evaluating the kiss. Probably.

Dan's other hand slides inside my jacket now and his fingers curl into my side, briefly, before his hand moves higher. His knuckles graze over my ribs and I sit up straighter, pulling my stomach in. He runs his tongue over my bottom lip and I realise I'm supposed to be doing something with mine. I run it along his lip and he sighs against my mouth as his fingers brush up against the side of my breast.

OK. He's heading for the boobs. I can do this. I can sit here in a public place and get felt up. That's absolutely fine. I just need to focus.

And then Dan's thumb brushes over my nipple and a few things happen at once. I inadvertently let out a sort of yelp and my leg shoots out under the table and connects with something soft. There's a squawk and a pigeon flies up between me and Dan. I screech and rear back in my seat, knocking into the table so that my beer falls over and rolls into Dan's lap.

Perfect.

CHAPTER TWENTY-TWO

Freya and Georgie are in the lounge when I get home. The TV's on, the lights are low, and there's a bottle of red and a bowl of crisps on the table.

'Soooooo?' Freya says, as soon as I walk in, pausing the TV. 'How did it go?' She's got her feet in Georgie's lap and Georgie's stroking her ankles.

'Great,' I say, flopping down on the other sofa. 'We're back at his place having sex right now.'

'Ha,' Freya says. 'You're funny.'

I close my eyes. 'I kicked a pigeon.'

'Is that a euphemism?' Freya says.

'Ha. No.' I open my eyes and shuffle on the seat, pulling a pair of balled socks out from behind my back. Ugh. Adam. 'I literally kicked a pigeon. Dan touched my boob, I kicked a pigeon, knocked over my lager and it poured into Dan's lap.'

Freya is just staring at me. 'Thank god you didn't try to have sex with him. You'd probably blow up a dog or something.'

Georgie snorts.

I drop my head back against the sofa. There was no way sex was on the agenda after the… pigeon incident. Dan was very polite about it, but still. It kind of killed the mood.

'How was it apart from that?' Georgie asks and Freya laughs.

'My stupid fucking shoes murdered my feet,' I say without opening my eyes. I had to prise them off as soon as I was in the front door and I almost threw them in the bin, but… they're so pretty. 'But other than that – and the pigeon – it was good. And he went and bought me socks.'

'Socks?' Freya says. 'You're never going to have sex.'

I straighten up and blink at her. 'What?'

'A man who wants to get into your knickers does not buy you socks.'

'I think you're wrong,' I tell her. 'He was very interested in my boobs. Well, one of them. Also, he was just being kind. Considerate. That's a good thing.'

'It's something,' she says. 'Was there more dull kissing?'

'There was more kissing,' I confirm. 'It wasn't dull.'

'The kissing's dull?' Georgie says, looking up at me from Freya's feet.

'Not dull!' I tell her. 'Freya just decided it was dull because I didn't hump him on Westminster Bridge. It was good.'

'Tingles this time?' Freya asks. 'A special feeling in your special place?'

'A bit,' I tell her.

And I'm not even lying. If I'd been able to shut my brain off enough to really pay attention then I feel like there definitely would have been tingles. Probably.

Freya swings her legs down and Georgie curls up against her side, one hand fisted in the front of Freya's ironic Guns N' Roses T-shirt. I know they'd both happily talk to me, but I also know I've interrupted their evening and they're probably dying to get back to watching whatever it is they're watching.

'What are you watching?' I ask, squinting at the TV.

'*The Sopranos*,' Freya says. 'Georgie's never seen it, can you believe?'

I can. 'Cos I haven't either.

'I think I'm just going to go and watch a romantic comedy on Netflix,' I say, clambering out of the chair and wincing at the pain in my feet. There's no way I'll be able to stand up all day tomorrow at work. I'll have to beg Henry to give me something I can do sitting down.

'That,' Freya says, pointing at me with her glass of wine, 'is part of your problem.'

'What is? And what problem?'

'You're a hopeless romantic!' she says.

'Aww,' Georgie murmurs, nuzzling into Freya's neck.

I need to get out of here; I know from painful experience that Freya has no boundaries where PDA is concerned.

'I know I am,' I say. Well, a romantic. I don't know about 'hopeless'. 'What's wrong with that?'

'It's fine. It's good. But you need a bit of realism too. You know, life is not all "I'm just a boy standing in front of a girl" it's more like "Here's a boy, in his pants, and they're not even clean, but somehow I love him anyway".'

I shake my head. 'I don't know if I could love a man in dirty pants.'

She grins. 'But you know what I mean? Romance isn't all big declarations, running to the airport, performing a song for you at the O2. Sometimes it's like… OK, I'll give you an example. Georgie came over the other night, right? And I'd told her that I like M&Ms and she brought me a family bag.'

'That's nice,' I say. 'It's not exactly romantic.'

'Well, then I kind of put them in places and it was all really fucking hot…'

Georgie giggles into Freya's neck.

'But that's not my point,' Freya continues. 'My point is that she listened to me, remembered something I'd said, and did something to make me happy. And then something to make me really horny.' She shakes her head. 'I've gone off the point a bit.'

Georgie's hand is creeping under Freya's T-shirt now. I edge towards the door.

'I know that romance in films and books isn't real,' I say. 'I'm not an idiot.'

'But do you? Because currently you're dating someone you don't even like because you think you had a recurring dream about him.'

Georgie looks over at me, her eyebrows shooting up.

'I did have a dream about him,' I tell her. 'And I do like him.'

'You like him, but you don't *like* like him,' Freya argues. 'And I worry that you're pinning too much on this. On the dream.'

I shake my head. 'I'm just optimistic, what's wrong with that?'

'Nothing's wrong with that. Of course it's not. But... it was a dream. Do you really think you have, like, psychic powers? Because... I don't know.'

'I don't... not exactly that. But I think I had the dream for a reason. I think I was meant to meet him. Dan,' I add for Georgie's benefit.

'And you're sure Dan was the man in your dream?'

'Yes.' I am. I think.

Freya looks at me with one eyebrow raised. 'Really? One hundred per cent?'

'I mean... I don't think I'm one hundred per cent about anything. Ever. Are you?'

'Yes,' she says. 'Loads of things.'

'Like?'

'Gravity.'

I roll my eyes. 'Things in your life, I mean. Like... when you moved to London. Were you one hundred per cent confident it would work out? Or your job. Were you one hundred per cent confident it was the right one? Or even the right career?'

'Maybe not. And no, I wasn't about any of those things you mentioned. But I was confident enough. I knew I wanted to live in London because it made me happy when I came here. Same with my job. It felt like the thing I should be doing.'

'She's a hundred per cent about me,' Georgie offers and Freya turns to kiss her.

I take the opportunity to try and escape from the room.

'Listen,' Freya says, turning on the sofa so she's facing me. 'I believe you had a dream and it had a big impact on you. I believe you think Dan was the man in your dream.'

'He was,' I say from the doorway. 'He is.'

She waves her hand dismissively. 'What if he's not? What if he's just a man you met in a park who's nice, but not right for you?'

'But he's—'

'If you're about to say "the man of my dreams" I'm gonna smash this glass and stab you with it.'

'I know,' I say. 'But he is.'

Freya shakes her head, but her face softens. 'Maybe you need bigger dreams.'

CHAPTER TWENTY-THREE

I'm in the park. It's busier than usual and quite noisy. At first I think it's full of people but as I walk further along the path, I realise it's full of pigeons. Pigeons in the trees and sitting on Dan's bench. Pigeons on the deckchairs and the bandstand. Pigeons squawking and fluttering and shitting everywhere. I see Dan in the distance and I dodge numerous pigeons until I get to him. He keeps walking until he's pressed right up against me. I slide my hands inside his jacket and as I lean in to kiss him, he pecks me instead.

And then I wake up.

*

'Have you talked to Mum?' Matt asks as soon as I answer my phone the following evening.

My heart plummets and bile rises in my throat. 'What's happened?'

'It's nothing bad, everyone's OK,' he says immediately. I wish he'd opened with that. 'I mean,' he continues. 'It's not great. But no one's dead. No one's ill.'

'Tell me,' I say. 'You're scaring me.'

'You OK?' Freya mouths at me across the living room, where she's marking. Again. I shrug and realise I'm blinking back tears.

'Tom's business is being investigated,' Matt says. 'Some accounting irregularities, apparently.'

My stomach lurches again. 'Stuff I've done?' I only record and categorise his expenses, but I know he uses the reports the software generates for tax and VAT.

'I think it's bigger than that,' he says. 'It may include stuff you've done, but that's not all.' I hear Matt suck in a breath and realise he's smoking. I thought he'd given up.

Freya comes over and squeezes my shoulder, then leaves the room.

'So what does it mean?' I ask Matt. 'What's happening?'

'They've had to stop trading. This accountancy firm's been instructed to, like, audit everything.'

'So what are they looking for? What do they think's happened?' I stare out through the window. It's been raining all day, but it just looks grey and miserable now.

'They think Tom's been taking money from the business. Like, for personal stuff.'

I shake my head. 'He's always really strict about that. He always makes sure any personal expenses are repaid. Once it was, like, a newspaper. It wasn't even a quid. But he paid it back.'

'Yeah,' Matt says. 'I think it's much bigger than that. We're talking thousands, not the odd quid for a paper or a coffee.'

'Wait,' I say – something in his voice is making me feel queasy. 'You don't think he really did this?'

Matt sighs. 'I don't know. I don't want to. But they don't do this kind of thing randomly. It seems like he might've done. Maybe not intentionally, but... yeah.'

'He wouldn't though,' I say, instantly. 'Tom's not dishonest. He's the most honest person I know. Remember that time at the cashpoint? Someone had left their cash? And he handed it in?'

'I know,' Matt says. 'It's unbelievable. Maybe he just fucked up somehow. It happens.'

Freya comes back and hands me a beer and I smile quickly at her before taking a long pull of it. I feel like I need something stronger: what do they give people for shock? Brandy. We haven't got any brandy.

'So what's happening now?' I ask Matt.

'He's at home. He's really pissed off. He thought he could carry on trading while they did the investigation and it was only when they turned up they told him he'd have to shut down. So there's like long-time clients he's had to let down.'

'That's not good.'

'Nope. I think his worry is that even if the investigation turns out in his favour, he'll have lost some important clients.'

'Shit! How long's it going to take?'

'Dunno. Could take months, apparently. I've been trying to find out, but it seems like it's a long as a piece of string type of thing, you know?'

'How's Mum?'

I wish I was at home. I'd feel better if I could hear what's happening from Tom, have Mum tell me it'll all be OK.

'Oh, you know Mum. She's furious. She thinks it's all a stitch-up. She asked him if he has any enemies.'

I laugh and then say, 'God. This is awful.'

'I know. But maybe it's not as bad as it seems. Maybe it'll turn out to be nothing.'

'I hope so.'

I ask him about work and life and Lydia, but he's his usual non-committal self, offering only short, not very informative answers. I feel like now that he's told me about Tom, he just wants to get off the phone. Eventually, I let him, after making him promise to ring me as soon as he knows anything.

'Don't worry,' he says just before hanging up.

Bit late for that now.

*

'You could ask Dan about it,' Freya says, once I've told her everything Matt's told me. 'Like what usually happens in this kind of situation. What the process is.'

'Do you think? I mean, he's not qualified yet.'

'No, but he's worked in accountancy, right? He's going to know more than we do, anyway.'

'That wouldn't be difficult.'

'I'm sure he could ask someone he works with.'

'He's still looking for work.' He had another interview today, actually. I need to text him and ask how it went.

'Well, someone he's worked with in the past then. Even knowing the right terms to Google. Worth a try.'

I nod. She's right. It definitely is.

'I'll text him,' I tell her.

CHAPTER TWENTY-FOUR

I'm walking up the stairs at the station and I can see Dan waiting for me at the top. It's bright outside so I can only see him in silhouette, his outline edged in gold. I get to the top and walk towards him, still sheltering my eyes against the sun, which is almost painfully bright. When I get there, it's not Dan. It's Henry.

'Oh hey!'

He smiles. 'Hi.'

'I wasn't expecting to see you here.'

'I thought I'd come and meet you.'

He turns and we both walk out into the street.

'I missed you,' Henry says.

I push him back against the wall and press my body up against his. And then I wake up.

*

'Are you nervous?' Freya asks me. She's sitting on my bed while I do my make-up in the long mirror that's glued to the wall. (And I know this because I tried to take it down when I first moved in.)

I shake my head. But I am. A bit. Also I still feel weird after dreaming about Henry. Again. I know it's just because I spend so much time with him and it's not like I haven't dreamt about him before, but I've never dreamt about *kissing* him before. That is very much new. I don't say any of this to Freya. I just carry on filling in my left eyebrow.

'It's a big step, meeting the friends,' she says. 'And you don't usually wear make-up to brunch.'

'He hasn't seen me without make-up yet. And he's already met Henry. And it wasn't a big deal when Georgie met us – she was naked the first time Henry saw her.'

'Meh,' she says. 'That's different.'

I start on the other eyebrow. 'Why is it?'

'Because Georgie's my girlfriend. But Dan is The Man of Your Dreams.' She says this in a portentous voice. Like a movie trailer voiceover.

'Oh god.' I turn and look at her. 'Please don't say that to him.'

'You still haven't told him?' She clasps her hands in front of her chest. 'That he is your destiny?'

'No. And you can't tell him either.' I drop the eyebrow pencil back in my make-up bag and take out my mascara.

'You know you do need to tell him at some point though, right?' Freya says. She's lying down on my bed now.

'Why do I?'

'Because!'

'Convincing argument.'

'Because if you are going to be together forever, you can't keep something like that from him. Literally the reason you asked him out! The reason you were in London! The reason you were lurking in the park like a creeper!'

'See, this is why I don't want to tell him.'

'And yet…'

'I know. Shut up. Not today though. He's got enough to deal with meeting you lot.'

'You make a good point,' she says, rolling onto her back. She hasn't bothered getting dressed up to meet him. She's wearing ripped jeans and a sweatshirt that she usually only wears when she's hungover or on her period. Her hair is in a high ponytail, she's wearing her glasses, not her contacts, and she still looks great. Annoying.

'When are you going to do something about this room?' she asks. 'You've seen the stain on the ceiling, right?'

'Yeah.' I put the mascara down and pout at myself in the mirror. 'I'm going to ask Henry to ask his dad to do something about that.'

'I could do the whole room,' Freya says. 'I'll do it for cost. It'll be fun.'

I decide I look as good as I'm going to look and zip up my make-up bag. 'Thanks, but I can't even afford the materials. And it doesn't matter anyway. I only really sleep in here, I don't need it to be fancy.'

'But if you're going to be bringing men back here…' She circles her hand over the duvet cover.

'It's not men, it's one man. And I really don't think Dan will care.'

'You're hopeless,' she says. 'You have to put in a bit of effort every now and then.'

'I have!' I say, fanning my hands underneath my chin and batting my eyelashes.

She stands up and kisses me quickly on the lips. 'And you look gorgeous. Let's go. I could eat the crotch out of a low-flying duck.'

*

Dan has Freya charmed within less than a minute. He's waiting outside Mr C's when we get there, introduces himself and shakes everyone's hand, and then makes a rubbish, but endearing, joke about being scared to meet everyone. As we walk into the cafe, Freya grins at me and gives me two thumbs up behind Dan's back. And then Mrs C comes over to take our order and says, 'Oh! Handsome boy!' and actually strokes his hair. He smiles at her and asks what she recommends on the menu and then actually orders it.

'Ohhhh,' she says to me. 'This one is a good one.'

He is. He is a good one. I would never have brought Anthony here. I didn't even introduce him to my friends. And if I'd known

Freya then, he one hundred per cent would have made a dodgy comment about lesbian sex and she'd have stabbed him with a fork.

'So how do you all know each other?' Dan asks, once we've all got drinks.

'From the house,' Adam tells him. 'Henry was there first and then Freya, and then me and Celine moved in. And then…' He clicks his fingers and points at me.

Dan smiles at me. 'And you all get on? That's good.'

'It took a while to get the right group though,' Henry says. 'We had some nightmares along the way.'

'Right,' Dan says. 'It's tough sharing with strangers.'

'Do you get on with your flatmates?' Henry asks him.

Dan's just taken a sip of coffee, so he nods, then swallows and says, 'They're great, yeah. I don't see much of them, which is good. They both work long hours. But they're tidy enough, you know? I've no complaints. Well, Anton never flushes the loo, but other than that.'

While we wait for our food, he chats with Adam about sport, asks Celine questions about her job – and not the stupid questions that wind her up, like whether she's ever shouted 'This whole court's out of order!' but actual interesting, insightful questions. He asks Henry about the bookshop, but it's a bit of a conversational dead end since Dan doesn't read. But then he and Freya realise they're both big horror film fans and get overexcited about some seventies remake that's about to hit cinemas.

Mrs C brings our food and then just stands there, smiling at Dan.

'Getting jealous here, Mrs C,' Adam says, raising one eyebrow at her.

She laughs and flutters and says, 'You are a bad boy.'

'You're an idiot,' Celine tells him, once Mrs C has gone.

'You won't get Bea to watch horror movies with you,' Freya tells Dan, reaching over and pinching a bit of his toast (which is how I know she likes him). 'She only watches romantic comedies.'

'I don't only watch romantic comedies,' I say, turning to see if I can spot Mrs C – I need another coffee, but I got distracted by her fussing over Dan and forgot to ask.

'What was the last film you watched that wasn't a romcom?' Freya asks me.

I frown, trying to remember. I try to mentally scroll Netflix. '*Mystic Pizza*!' I say, eventually. 'And *Legally Blonde*! They're not romcoms. You're a *Legally Blonde* fan, right, Henry?'

'Who isn't?' Henry says and I grin at him. I think he's actually more of a Reese Witherspoon fan, but still.

'Eh, they're chick flicks though,' Dan says.

'Ugh,' I manage to catch Mrs C's eye and she waves and heads back over. 'I hate that expression. Exactly what in either of them makes them inappropriate for men? Feelings? Don't men have feelings?'

'I don't,' Adam says. 'Not from the waist up anyway.'

I look around the table for something to throw at him and have to make do with a rolled up sugar sachet wrapper. He just grins at me.

'I don't know what your problem is,' Adam says. 'Chick flicks for the ladies – about feelings and love and… shoes. And dick flicks for the men: explosions, sex, guns and cars.'

'No sex for the ladies?' Freya asks him, one eyebrow raised. (Celine is ignoring him. She's on her phone.)

'You can have a bit of sex—' Adam says.

'Ooh, can I?' Mrs C replies, arriving at the table. 'Do you want me now or will you finish breakfast first?'

We all laugh and Adam does something I've never seen him do before: he blushes.

'Oh my god,' Celine says, turning in her seat. 'You are bright red.'

She quickly takes a photo and Adam roars at her before grabbing her wrist and trying to take the phone. She still hasn't told him about the baby. She says she's working up to it. She'll know when it's the right time.

While the two of them wrestle, I order another coffee from Mrs C and she winks at me before she goes.

*

Dan comes back to the house with me. With all of us. But as soon as we're through the door, the others disperse to their rooms. I think about just taking Dan to the living room, but I know that would end up being weird because the others would pop in and out, so instead I take him up to my room. I'm conscious all the way up the stairs that we're going to my room. Where my bed is. Where there actually isn't much more than my bed. Me and Dan in a room full of bed.

'Your friends are really great,' he says, as soon as the door is closed behind us.

'They are,' I agree. 'And you were a big hit. Especially with Mrs C.'

He laughs, his eyes crinkling. 'How lovely is she?'

Freya and I have actually talked about a Mrs C test in the past – if you introduce someone to Mrs C and they don't think she's wonderful, the relationship can go no further. Dan has passed with flying colours.

'So this is your room,' Dan says then.

We're both still just standing there. I feel like the bed is glowing or flashing arrows.

'Yep. Sorry there's, um, nowhere to sit.'

I sit down tentatively on the edge of the bed. 'It's really boring, I know. Freya keeps offering to decorate it for me, but I don't see the point, it's so small.'

'It's nice,' Dan lies, looking around.

I wish I had one of those beds that folds down from the wall, so there could be a clear line between not bed and bed. We could sit and talk and maybe watch a film and then if we decided we wanted to have sex… ta-da! Bed! A film does seem like a good idea though. Better than just contemplating the bed.

'Do you want to watch a film or something?' I ask. 'Not horror.'

He sits next to me, smiling. 'Or something.'

Oh. Ta-da!

'Not if you don't—' he says, instantly.

'No, I do.' I don't. 'We can. But can I just ask you about something first?'

First. Yikes. First I ask you the thing and then we have the sex. Probably.

He turns ninety degrees so he's looking at me. 'Course.'

And the thing is, he means it. He's happy to wait. To listen to whatever it is I want to talk about. And while that shouldn't seem like that big a deal, it sort of feels like it is. I wanted security and safety. The dream promised me security and safety. And I feel incredibly safe with Dan. He reminds me of Tom. And I really don't want to be thinking about Tom when I'm about to have sex. (Probably.)

I tell him everything I know about Tom's business and what Matt's told me.

'And you're worried that you could be implicated?' he says, when I've finished.

'Um. A bit? But mostly I'm worried about what's going to happen to Tom. I mean, he's been building that business for years – it's like his baby – and... I mean, I don't know where the Revenue have got their information from... Could someone report something like this maliciously? Like a business rival?'

He frowns. 'From what you've told me, it sounds like it's gone past that point. Something like that would come out in preliminary investigations, I think.'

'So you think there's actually something there? Something wrong?'

He stretches his shoulders back and I hear his neck crack. 'I couldn't say without actually looking into it. But I can definitely have a look at Companies House – their accounts, tax returns, that sort of thing. And I'll see if I know anyone who's working on it.'

'That would be great. Thank you.'

'Are you still working for him?'

I shake my head. 'I haven't done anything since Matt told me what was happening. But I was until a couple of weeks ago, yeah.'

'OK, so the first thing I'd say is to double-check all your work, to make sure there are no errors there. It's bookkeeping you do, right?'

I nod.

'So if you've maybe got a bit… generous about allowances – including things you know really shouldn't be included, that sort of thing – now's the time to sort that. Unless they've already been submitted. And it's too late.'

'I was part way through a report,' I say, trying to think of the receipts Tom had sent me and when I'd stopped checking them against the Revenue website. Basically, if Tom sends me receipts, I include them. I've never questioned anything.

'So have a look back over that,' Dan says. 'And I'll see what I can find out. OK?'

'OK,' I say.

There's a knot in my stomach. What if Tom really has done something that's going to get him into trouble? Not on purpose – I know he would never do that – but what if he's missed something or just cocked up in some way, he'd be—

Dan picks my hand up off the duvet and threads his fingers between mine.

Oh.

'Try not to worry,' he says. 'It's probably a misunderstanding.'

'Sorry,' I say. 'That wasn't sexy.'

'Oh, I don't know,' he says, dropping his forehead down onto my shoulder. 'Accountancy chat gets me hot.'

I laugh – I remember thinking exactly that the first time I met him – and turn slightly towards him.

'It's embarrassing at work sometimes. Show me a well-balanced column and I'm anyone's.'

'Anyone's?' I say, as his lips graze my neck.

'Just yours right now.'

I turn and brush my lips across his cheek. It's stubbly and warm and he smells really good. He tips his head up so his lips meet mine and I sink into the kiss. I'm on my bed. Kissing Dan. I'm kissing Dan on my bed. I really need to get my brain to shut the fuck up this time.

I slide one hand up around the back of his neck, my thumb brushing over his earlobe, and he smiles into the kiss, which makes me smile. This is good and nice. I can totally do this. The condoms are in my bedside drawer, I'm wearing good underwear, I've shaved my legs. Today could be the day. Today should be the day.

Dan's hand moves up to rest on my hip and I slide down the bed a little so he can push up against me. He's hard already, I can feel it against my hip and I shift myself again so he's pressing between my legs. This definitely feels good. I can work with this. Dan groans and my hips jerk back involuntarily.

'You OK?' he whispers.

'Yeah. Sorry. It's just… I can hear when Adam and Celine do it, so I don't want—'

'That's OK,' he says, dipping his head and curling his tongue into the hollow of my throat. 'I can be quiet.'

He moves down the bed, shuffling me with him, until he's lying on top of me, his dick pressed between my legs. I curl my hips up so I'm rubbing against him and it's good. It feels familiar. More like when I touch myself than when I slept with Anthony.

Anthony would've been done by now. He didn't really care about whether I enjoyed it or not. And I never really did.

Dan's pushing my top up now, his fingers sliding over my ribs. I look up and see the stain on my ceiling. I really do need to speak to Henry about that. I close my eyes. I shouldn't be thinking about Henry right now. Dan is literally on top of me. That's just bad manners. I think about the dream. How I pushed Henry back against the wall and pressed my body against him. Dan grinds his hips, and I gasp. He's kissing along my collarbones now, his hand brushing over my left boob. I need to stop thinking about Henry. I need to focus on Dan. I shiver and hook one leg around his, pressing him more firmly against me.

A door slams downstairs and I wonder who it is. I don't think any of them would actually come into the room, but it's a bit nerve-wracking to know that they're all walking around as normal while I'm doing this. I picture them all in the kitchen: Celine complaining about the dishes, Freya sexting Georgie, Adam watching the football, Henry making a cup of tea, all of them listening out for any noises Dan and I might make. That's not what they'll be doing – they've probably forgotten Dan's even here – but... what if they are? I don't want Henry to hear me having sex. Why am I still even thinking about Henry?

Dan's hand is moving under my bra now, pushing it up over my boob, his thumb brushing over my nipple. I hook my other leg around him, shifting my hips until his dick is perfectly positioned. I wonder if I could come like this. I never came like this with Anthony. I never came with Anthony at all.

Dan's tongue flickers over my nipple and I arch my back.

'This OK?' he murmurs.

I moan in response and again think about my friends in their rooms, potentially listening. They won't be listening. Probably. Why am I still thinking? I want to stop thinking.

Dan sucks my nipple into his mouth and I dig my fingers into his shoulders. We're really doing this. I'm going to come like this and then we'll take our clothes off and then we'll have sex. Here. Now. Where Henry can hear us.

I can't do it.

'Dan,' I say, shifting my hips away from his dick.

'Hmmm?' He's pretty busy with my nipple. I kind of want to shove his head off, but that would be rude.

I unhook my legs and shift my hips again, dislodging him.

'Dan?' Louder this time.

'You OK?' he says. He tips his chin up and rests his face on my boob to look up at me. He's really cute. But I really don't want to have sex with him. I could. And it would probably be good – he's sweet and considerate and I'm sure he'd make it good for me – but it wouldn't be right. It just wouldn't.

'I'm sorry,' I say. 'I can't do this.'

He pushes himself up on his arms. He's got really good arms. 'No?'

'No. I'm sorry. I don't know why. I just—'

'We don't have to have sex,' he says. His mouth is red and looks swollen. I wish I wanted to kiss it. 'I could go down on you? Or get you off like this? I thought you were close, maybe.'

'I think that still counts as sex,' I say. 'And I can't. I'm sorry.'

He rolls off me, but leaves his arm across my waist. 'Can I ask why?'

I stare up at the ceiling again. 'It's too soon, I think. My last boyfriend…' I squeeze my eyes shut and then open them again, glancing down at him before looking back up at the ceiling. 'I've only had one boyfriend. And he wasn't nice. And I just… I feel like I need to take this a bit slower.'

'You should've told me,' he says, bumping his head against my shoulder. 'I hope you didn't feel pressured or anything.'

I squeeze his forearm. 'No. You're great, honestly. I'm sorry I didn't tell you.'

'Do you still know this guy? Want me to rough him up for you?'

I laugh. 'No. He ghosted me. Ages ago now.'

'What. A. Dick.'

I laugh again. God, I can't remember ever laughing about Anthony before. But he was a dick. He absolutely was.

'You rough people up?' I ask, smiling.

'Well, I never have before. But I could totally give it a go.'

I turn my head so I can kiss him on the forehead. 'Thank you.'

'Ooh,' he says, shuffling up to the pillow. 'Forehead kiss. That's not good.'

'It was the only bit of you I could reach!' I say.

He kisses my temple. 'I was only joking. You're OK, yeah?'

I nod. 'I'm good. Thanks for understanding.'

'Oh, no worries.' We lie in silence for a few seconds and then Dan says, 'You haven't got an en suite have you?'

'No, sorry. But the bathroom's next door.'

'No,' he says. 'That's OK. Just got a bit of a situation. In my pants.'

CHAPTER TWENTY-FIVE

'Do you have any books about guinea pigs?'

The boy looks about thirteen and is wearing a red hoodie, purple T-shirt and round glasses. He's been lurking in the shop for about ten minutes, and approached the desk twice and changed his mind at the last minute, before finally asking the question.

'Fiction or non-fiction?' I ask him.

He frowns. 'I think… fiction?'

I walk around the counter and show him over to the children's section.

'I'm pretty sure we've got *Olga da Polga*,' I tell him. 'Have you read that one?'

He doesn't say anything, so I look up and see him shaking his head. He's biting his lip, nervously.

'It might be a bit young for you,' I tell him. 'But it's good. Funny. I read it when I was little.'

I go back to the counter, leaving him looking at the book, and before too long he comes back again.

'Do you have any books about looking after guinea pigs?'

'Actually, I'm not sure.' I call Henry over and ask him and he takes the boy over to look in the animals section.

When he leaves – after buying the guinea pig care book, but not *Olga da Polga* – Henry joins me behind the counter.

'Was that Harry Potter?'

I laugh. 'No. No scar.'

'Well… he had a fringe.'

'True. But also Harry Potter would be in his thirties now.'

'Shut up!' Henry says.

'Nope. He really would.'

'God.' Henry leans down and rests his head on the counter. 'That's the worst thing I've heard all day. And I had to listen to Celine puking this morning. I can't believe she still hasn't told Adam.'

'I know,' I say. 'She says she's waiting for the right time.'

Henry shakes his head. 'I guess she knows him better than we do.'

'She might be waiting for him to work it out himself,' I suggest.

Henry laughs. 'Good luck with that.'

I smile. 'I know. But you never really know how other people's relationships work, do you?' And then I ask him something I've been wondering about. 'If me and Dan came into the shop, what would you say?' I ask Henry, who is still fiddling in the till drawer.

'What?'

'You know what I mean. If you were working and me and Dan came in, as a couple, would you say we'd stay together or split?'

'I wouldn't say anything because you wouldn't be here to say it to.'

'Henry.'

'Bea.'

'You know what I mean.'

He groans, slamming the till drawer shut. 'OK. If Bea One came in here with Dan and Bea Two was standing here with me, bored, and probably fiddling with her phone that she's not meant to have on the shop floor… I think I'd say they looked good together. You looked good together, I mean. You and Dan.'

'But it's not just about how we look, is it? It's about how we interact. What did you think at brunch? I know you thought something. You're super judgemental.'

He smiles, rubbing his hand over his face. 'I am not.'

'Tell me please. I won't be offended. Probably.'

He drops his head back, looking up at the ceiling, and then straightens up again. 'OK. Well. He's nice. He seems like a nice bloke.'

'He is.'

'Right. But… I'm not really feeling the two of you together.'

'Why not?' I know why I think he's not right, but I really want to know why Henry thinks he's not right.

'You just don't… you seem more like friends. But maybe not even friends. Maybe colleagues.'

'Really? How?'

'Ugh, god, I should've agreed to just one question.' He grabs the edge of the desk and bends over, stretching his shoulders. 'OK. So. Like Celine and Adam tease each other. They take the piss and wind each other up. Yeah?'

I nod.

'And Freya and Georgie can't keep their hands off each other.'

This is also true.

'Even, like, Mr and Mrs C… they're affectionate. They're cute together, you know? You and Dan are just… you're like – who's the guy in *Sleepless in Seattle*?'

'Tom Hanks?'

'Duh. No. The one she's engaged to. Meg Ryan.'

'When did you watch *Sleepless in Seattle*?'

'It's my mum's favourite film. I've watched it loads of times.'

'So you should know who you're talking about then?'

He rolls his eyes at me. 'I can never remember his name. Whatever. He's engaged to Meg Ryan—'

'Annie.'

'Annie. God. Right, so he's engaged to Annie, but she's not that into him. And then she meets Tom Hanks and… you know.'

'So you're saying I should try to meet Tom Hanks?' I grin at him.

'I think he's a bit old for you. Although he has written a book, have you seen—'

'Walter.'

'What?'

'Annie's fiancé is Walter.'

'Right. Bill Paxton.'

'Pullman.'

'Is it?'

'Yeah. Bill Paxton died. He was the guy in *Twister*. And *Titanic*. And *Weird Science*.'

'And Bill Pullman's the President in *Independence Day*, right?'

'Yes.' I glance over at the door as a customer comes in. 'He's also the guy she chooses in *While You Were Sleeping*.'

'I don't think I've seen that one,' Henry says, stepping out from behind the counter. 'Fancy a tea?'

'Please. And you should watch it. At Christmas. It's a good Christmas film.'

'I'll put it in my diary,' he says, as he disappears into the kitchen.

The customer comes over and asks for recommendations of exciting books for a non-reader. It's only when she's gone that Henry brings my tea.

'You're not upset,' he says, without looking at me. 'About what I said?'

'Getting Bill Pullman and Bill Paxton confused? Nah, I think it's pretty common.'

'Not that. What I said about you and Dan.'

I take a breath. 'No. I mean it's still pretty new. We're getting to know each other. And… it's different when we're in public.'

Henry goes pink. 'I'm sure.'

I almost want to tell him. That even though me and Dan were in my room, nothing happened. Well, not nothing. But not what he presumably thinks happened. But there's no way I can talk to him about it. And he probably wouldn't even care. But I do need to talk to someone.

❈

'I'm getting grapefruit gin,' Freya says, squinting up at the blackboard menu in the cafe above the cinema. The film doesn't start for another hour, but we made sure to get here early because the bar is so nice.

'God,' I say. 'Put your glasses on.'

'Not until the lights go off,' she says. 'What are you getting?'

'I'll have the same, I think.'

'Ooh,' she says, stepping up to the counter. 'Hitting the hard stuff. What's up?'

'I need to talk to you about something. What cakes are there? I want cake too.'

'Gin *and* cake? Have you killed someone?'

'Funny. I'll go and get a table.'

I head for the far corner under the window, but Freya shouts, 'Go outside! The sun's shining!'

I push open the French doors and step out onto the balcony. I love it so much – it's above the marquee and behind the sign with the film titles on, so it's very cool, but it's almost always too hot. Not that Freya cares. When she joins me, she's already wearing a pair of huge sunglasses.

'Are they prescription?'

'Course,' she says, putting the tray down on the table. 'I wouldn't be able to see otherwise.'

'Doesn't usually stop you.'

She sits down next to me and takes an enormous gulp of her gin, before saying, 'So. What's up?'

I glance around. There's one other person sitting out here – a man at the far end, also wearing sunglasses and reading the *Telegraph*. I lean closer to Freya.

'So. I tried to have sex with Dan. And I couldn't do it.'

'Why not? It's easy. Even I've done it. And I'm a lesbian.' She enunciates the last word and the man at the other end of the balcony rattles his newspaper.

'I think…' I say. And then I take a swig of my own gin. 'I think maybe I don't fancy him enough. Or like him enough, maybe?'

'Don't you know?'

I sigh. 'No? I mean, he's great. He's kind. And he's funny. A bit. And he's hot, right?'

'Les-bi-an,' she says again.

'Oh shut up, I know you know he's hot.'

'He's hot.'

'Right. So why am I just… not that into him?'

'Is that a genuine question? Like, do you want me to actually answer that? For real? No bullshit?'

'Yes.' I pick up my gin, put it down again, shove a forkful of cake into my mouth.

Freya pushes her sunglasses up on her head and leans over so her face is right in front of mine. 'He's not the man of your dreams. You want him to be, but he's not. He's nice, you're nice, everything's fine, but there's no spark.'

'There was a bit of a spark,' I say. And drink some gin. 'Like…' I lean even closer so I'm speaking directly into her ear. 'I nearly came. When we were, like, dry humping or whatever. I mean, I felt like maybe I could've done.'

'Oh my god.' She leans back in her chair and looks at me. 'That doesn't mean anything. All that means is that your parts like his parts. And that is not something to base a relationship on. Like… I once had a wank watching Jeremy Kyle. Does that mean I want to do Jeremy Kyle? One hundred per cent not. You really cannot take relationship advice from your fanny.'

The man snaps his newspaper closed and goes inside.

'Repressed,' Freya says. 'He should have a chat with his dick.'

I drink some more gin.

'I've got a question,' Freya says. 'Why are you still going out with him?'

I close my eyes and wait for the sun to shine through my eyelids. 'He's nice.'

'Nice.'

'Nice is good.'

'Nice is blah. And he is nice. I liked him. But even I could see there wasn't much going on there. Between you. You were like friends.'

'That's what Henry said.'

'Did he now.'

I open my eyes. 'What does that mean?'

'Nothing.' She's got her sunglasses on again. 'Just interesting that Henry noticed too. That's all.'

I drink some more gin, looking down on the street below. I love it here. I love that there are still independent shops. Just from where I'm sitting I can see a Polish deli, an Italian cafe, and a florist whose owner I know is French because I ordered birthday flowers for my mum from there. The scents of all the cafes and delis mix together along with the coffee from the various coffee shops (and the car and bus fumes) and I think it might be my favourite scent in the world. I breathe in deeply (and hope the pollution doesn't kill me).

'Do you want to know what I think?' Freya says.

'That's why I asked.'

'I think you're scared. Because of Anthony. I think Anthony fucked you up and so now you want something safe – that's what you always say when you talk about the dream, isn't it? You feel safe and secure?'

'But that's normal, isn't it? Everyone wants to feel safe and secure?'

'Of course. But it depends on your reasons. Safety and security are great when someone makes you happy. When you want to tell them your secrets and, you know, give them your heart to take care of. Not when you want them to keep you safe because you're afraid. Or because someone else hurt you and you don't want to risk getting hurt again. Love is about taking risks.'

I stare at a bike courier as he weaves between cars.

'I'm scared,' I tell Freya.

She reaches over and squeezes my arm. 'I know you are. But Dan is not the man of your dreams. And you need to let that dream go.'

I know she's right. Or at least, I think she is. But what if she's wrong? What if I'm not scared because of Anthony? What if I'm scared of Dan? Of Dan being the man of my dreams. I can't give up on him – on the dream – just yet. I just can't.

CHAPTER TWENTY-SIX

I'm in the park. It's dark and there's music playing from the band-stand. I walk over to the bench and Dan's sitting there, but he's not in his usual black jeans and jacket; in fact he seems to be naked. I can't tell for sure because he's got a sheet wrapped around his waist. He looks at me.

'Come here.'

I can't move. I stare at him, but I actually want to turn and run the other way. Instead, I take a couple of steps towards him. My legs feel heavy and I feel like there's a rock inside my chest.

'Come on,' he says, patting the bench next to him.

I'm almost there – he's smiling at me and starting to lower the sheet – when I turn and run.

And then I wake up.

*

The following evening after work, I'm settling down with a cup of tea and a plate of toast – Adam's meant to be cooking, but he's not home yet – and a plan to half-watch *Letters to Juliet* (again), while also Googling 'accidental embezzlement' and 'companies in liquidation investigation', when my phone buzzes with a text from Dan: *GOT THE JOB!* followed by another that's just smiley faces and beers. And then, *Having a party. You have to come!*

What? I send. *Now?* I want to say 'On a Tuesday?!' but even I know that will make me sound ancient, so I don't. But on a Tuesday though?

He replies with three cry/laugh emojis.

I don't know whether that means 'of course' or 'of course not'. I show it to Freya, but she's no help.

I'm trying to formulate a response when the phone rings and Dan's name comes up.

'Tonight!' he says, as soon as I answer. 'Now!'

'OK,' I say, even though I'm already thinking that I'll have to shower and find something to wear and go back out again when I've mentally committed myself to the sofa. 'Congratulations!'

'It's a really good firm,' he says and I can hear him smiling. 'The one I wanted but didn't think I'd actually get. The money's good and the offices are amazing and… so can you come?'

I don't really want to. But I don't know how to explain it to myself, never mind him, so I tell him yes, of course.

*

On the Tube to Euston, I think about what happened – or rather didn't happen – after brunch. I've been thinking about it pretty much constantly, but mostly while doing other things. On the Tube, I can just sit and stare at my wan reflection in the window opposite and really focus on it. With the result that I spend fifteen minutes squirming with embarrassment and by the time I have to change at Euston, I really haven't come up with anything beyond 'I didn't really want to have sex with him'.

On the walk between the Northern line and the Victoria line, I idly wonder about writing a pros and cons list. Dan is lovely. He's kind to me. He was cool when I stopped the sex and while he shouldn't get cookies for that, I can't help mentally assigning him some because Anthony would not have been cool with it. I don't want to think about Anthony. But the thing is… no matter what Freya says, nice is important. Kindness is important. And Dan is literally the man of my dreams. Or he was. Whereas Henry – I don't want to think about Henry. If I did write a pros and cons list, the pros would be longer. A lot longer. But then cons. The cons would probably be weightier.

On the Victoria line I don't get a seat and I end up perched on one of those padded shelf things by the door between carriages. The windows are open and my hair is whipped around my head in a frenzy. My mind doesn't feel much better. Dan is perfect. He's my dream man. So I didn't want to have sex with him yesterday – doesn't mean I never will. Maybe we'll do it tonight. At the party. I think I've still got the condoms in my bag.

*

'I really didn't think so many people would come!' Dan tells me, taking my coat and hanging it up on a hook in the hall, just behind the door. 'Did you find it OK?'

'I found Brixton OK, the flat was a bit trickier.' Although I manage to find it by noise alone in the end. Didn't think anyone else would be playing 'Wild Thoughts' at such an outrageous volume on a Tuesday night.

'Yeah,' he says, glancing over his shoulder. I don't think he was listening. 'Come through and I'll get you a drink.'

I follow him into the small, dark, kitchen. There's a window but it's facing a brick wall. A youngish guy with curly floppy hair and a bit of a feeble goatee half-leers at me and Dan says, 'That's Anton.'

I raise a hand in a sort of wave and Anton high-fives it.

'Beer OK?' Dan asks me. He's already holding out a bottle of a brand I don't recognise. He looks a bit pink and sweaty and even giddier than usual. I wonder if he's high, but I think it's his usual enthusiasm.

'Fine, yeah.' I take it and immediately take a sip. It's more bitter than I'd usually drink, but it's not terrible.

'I'll introduce you to everyone,' Dan says. 'Actually, first…'

He tugs me slightly down the hallway, presses me against the wall and kisses me. He tastes like beer but it's nice.

'I'm really happy for you,' I tell him.

He grins at me and his eyes are glittering. 'I'm so excited. It's just the best thing that could've happened. Now come and meet everyone.'

He takes my hand and leads me through to the lounge: a long rectangle leading out onto a small balcony. White walls with a framed poster of New York I know is from IKEA and what looks like someone's lecture notes stuck up with Sellotape. It is full of people.

Dan points at his friends and shouts names and I know there's no chance of me remembering any of them. I smile and nod and occasionally laugh if it seems warranted. There are way more men here than women, but there are a couple of women who look to be about my age, sitting on a big squashy sofa at the end of the room.

'Anton's girlfriend,' Dan says, pointing at the one on the left, who has a pointy face, a chin-length bob, and is wearing the Tatty Devine Lobster necklace. He points at the other one. 'I don't know you.'

'Gemma,' she shouts and smiles at us both. She's got dyed silver hair with black roots and she's wearing bright red lipstick that I can see smeared around the neck of her beer bottle.

'Are you OK here for a minute?' Dan asks me. 'I just need to…' He gestures back at the door.

I nod and watch him walk back through the room, doing that handshake shoulder-grab thing men do, throwing his head back to laugh at something someone says, pretending to hit someone else in the balls.

He is mine, I think to myself. *He is meant for me. He is the man of my dreams.*

'How do you know Dan?' the girl closest to me – Gemma – asks.

'We only just met really,' I tell her.

'This isn't your first date?' the other girl says. I realise Dan didn't tell me her name, just that she was Anton's girlfriend.

I shake my head. 'No. We've had dinner. Also, we went on the London Eye and I had a panic attack.'

'Oh, that was you?' she says. 'I heard about that. You didn't know you were scared of heights?'

I shake my head. 'No! I've always been fine before.'

'That happened to me,' Gemma says. 'I went on a hen night to Blackpool and we went up the tower and there's this glass floor, right? And everyone else thought it was really funny to like jump on it – we were bladdered – and I just froze. I literally couldn't even move my legs. It took them ages to coax me out of there. They were all really pissed off with me.'

Anton's girlfriend is looking between me and Gemma curiously, as if she's never heard of such a thing.

'Kasie did a parachute jump,' Gemma tells me, gesturing to Anton's girlfriend with her thumb. 'She doesn't know what we're talking about.'

'It was fucking awesome,' Kasie said. 'I just… I don't really worry about things like that. The London Eye's safe, right? You can't fall off. It's not going to fall over or roll away.'

I picture it rolling along the Embankment and I have to grab the back of the sofa the two of them are sitting on.

'Shut up, Kase,' Gemma says. 'You're giving her the shits.'

I drink some of the weird beer. 'I'm OK. How long have you and Anton been together?'

While she tells me – they were at school together and went out and split up a lot, but then got back together when they both came to London – I glance up now and then hoping to see Dan. But there's no sign of him. I think at one point I hear his laugh, but I'm not sure I know it well enough to make a proper positive identification.

Kasie finishes her story, I finish my beer, and say 'I'm going to go and get another. You want anything?'

Kasie holds up a floral hip flask. 'I'm OK, ta.'

'I wouldn't mind another beer,' Gemma says, smiling.

The flat is now so full that it takes me a while to push my way through the crowd, apologising, smiling, at one point getting grabbed by some guy who's mistaken me for someone else. Eventually I make it to the kitchen, which is almost as crammed as the living room. Anton's sitting on the countertop with a glass of something dark. Dan's leaning against the cupboards talking to a really handsome black guy in a pink polo shirt.

'Hey!' he says when he sees me. 'You need another drink?'

'Please. And one for Gemma too.'

Dan twists round and then back, holding out two bottles of the same beer.

'She's great, isn't she? Kasie? I knew you'd like her.'

*

I'm just heading back into the scrum of the main room when I feel hands on my waist.

'Hey,' Dan says again, but gently this time, and almost directly into my ear. 'Wait here. I'll drop those off.'

He takes the beers and immediately shoves his way through the crowd. He took my beer. Also, last time he told me to wait for a bit he didn't come back. It wasn't exactly for long, but I don't know anyone and I kind of thought I'd come to spend time with him, even if it is a party.

But then Dan's back, sliding his hand into mine. His fingers are cold and damp from the beer. He tugs me in the opposite direction to the front door and I let him lead me past people I haven't seen before.

Someone I don't see properly says, 'Wheyyyy, Dan! Who's this?'

But then Dan pushes open a door and I follow him into a bedroom.

'My room,' he says, turning round and smiling at me.

'Wow.' The room is small, square. There's a single bed pushed up against the wall under a large window. There's a small chest of drawers and one of those fabric wardrobes in the corner opposite the bed. Otherwise it's totally plain. Plainer than mine. At least I've got a mirror.

Music from the other room is bleeding through the wall and someone shouts 'Come on, ya dickhead!' from the hall.

'Do you want to go back out there?' Dan asks.

I laugh. 'It's your party.'

He shrugs. 'I can take a break from hosting. I've wanted to see you.' He takes a couple of steps back and sits on the bed. 'Do you want to?'

I'm not exactly sure what he's asking me. Do I want to sit? Do I want to do more? I figure I'll start with sitting and see where it goes. I sit.

'I'm glad you came,' he says, reaching over and sliding his fingers between mine.

'Me too,' I say.

He leans forward and I look at his mouth just before he presses it to mine. He's got a nice mouth, nice lips. His tongue slides across my bottom lip and he's already starting to lean over a bit too much, I'm tipping back towards his pillow. So not just kissing then. More than kissing. That's OK. I let him lower me to the bed and he's lying next to me, between me and the wall. If I wanted to, I could swing my legs off the bed and leave. But I don't want to. Do I?

'Bea,' he says, against my neck. 'I really like you. Can I tell you something?'

'Mm-hmm.'

'I was kind of testing you. Out there.'

He pushes himself up so he's smiling down at me. I look back at him.

'Testing me how?'

'I sort of left you on your own a bit on purpose. To see how you'd get on.'

'OK,' I say. I know I'm frowning. I can't help it.

'I've had girlfriends before who were kind of clingy, you know? I want to be with someone independent. Who doesn't need to be, like, hanging off me all the time.'

A test. I really don't like the idea of a test. But I know I can be clingy. Anthony used to call me clingy. And brunch was a test, wasn't it? And meeting Mrs C. I'm not wild about it, but I guess it makes sense.

'Is that cool?' Dan says. 'I wouldn't usually, it's just… I really like you.'

'I like you,' I say. 'It's fine.'

He dips his head back down and licks behind my ear. It feels weird and I almost shudder but have to suppress it. I shift slightly on the bed so his face is closer to my collarbones. I liked it when he kissed them last time. He can do that again. Instead, he moves up to kiss me again, his tongue pressing in further, curling and stroking. I realise I'm not doing anything with mine, so I slide it against his and immediately pull back.

'Sorry,' I tell him. 'Couldn't breathe.'

He smiles down at me. 'You look so good.'

I stare up at him. I've seen him in my head for so long. I've dreamed about him – about this – for so long. So why am I thinking about making a run for it?

'Is this OK?' he says again, as he slides his hand under the silky kimono top I'm wearing.

I nod. Which doesn't really work since he's kissing me again. 'S'fine,' I say against his mouth.

His hand keeps sliding upwards and I realise I could do the same. I curl my fingers under the hem of his T-shirt and graze my fingertips against his skin. It's soft and warm and I flatten my hands, sliding them higher. I can feel his muscles flexing and relaxing as he moves against me. And suddenly I can't breathe.

'Wait a sec,' I say, turning my head. 'You're squashing me.'

'Fuck,' he says, immediately raising himself off me. 'I'm sorry.'

'If you lie down...' I suggest.

He rolls off me and lies on his back, smiling up at me. 'Better?'

I push his T-shirt up over his stomach. He's got a six-pack. And a line of dark hair from the centre of his chest, disappearing into the waistband of his jeans. I lean down and kiss it and Dan shudders.

'S'good,' he says.

'Yeah?'

He pushes one hand into my hair. I keep kissing, up towards his chest. He smells really good. I flick my tongue over his nipple and he groans, gripping my waist.

'Come up here.'

I slide my body up his and kiss him gently.

'You want to stay?' he whispers.

'Not tonight,' I say. 'I've got work in the morning.' Because it's a fucking Tuesday.

'Yeah,' he says, glancing over towards the door. 'You're right. But soon, yeah?'

I kiss him again. 'Yeah. Soon.'

CHAPTER TWENTY-SEVEN

'What are you doing?' I ask Henry, as soon as I walk into the living room. Or try to. I can't actually get in because the sofa's been pushed backwards and it's blocking the doorway.

'Oh hey!' He looks up at me and smiles. His cheeks are pink and his fringe is sticking to his forehead sweatily. 'You're back early. What happened to the party?'

'Nothing. It was fine,' I say. 'Seriously. What are you doing?'

Along with the shifted sofa, the coffee table and armchair have been moved to the other side of the room. In the space between lie a bunch of instructions and a quite ridiculous number of piles of screws and nails. They all look very well ordered though, in neat groups.

'Well, this was meant to be a surprise,' Henry says. 'But you've ruined it.'

He pushes his hand back through his hair and it sticks up in tufts for a second before settling back down.

'I'm making you a bookcase.'

'Seriously?' I say. I've been talking about getting a bookcase forever. I clamber over the back of the sofa and drop down onto it to look at him more closely.

'Yeah.' He looks down at some sheets of paper on the floor by his legs. 'It's just not going so well.'

'Why are you building me a bookcase?'

He glances up, looking confused, and then down again. He pokes at a pile of nails with his finger.

'You've been saying for ages that you were going to get one. And that tower of books on your bedside table is a health and safety issue. So as your landlord—'

'Shut up!' I interrupt. 'This is amazing! I was totally going to order one myself. I'll pay you back for this one.'

'You shut up,' he says, smiling at me. 'Definitely don't want payment. Might need a bit of help with building it though. It's not as easy as it looks. There are like a hundred of these.'

He holds up a tiny white plastic disc.

'What are they even for?'

'Not sure.' He turns one of the pieces of paper over, frowning down at it, and then hands it to me. 'You read it. I'm sure we can work it out between us.'

I read through the instructions – the little discs are to cover the screw heads – and then direct Henry as he starts the actual building.

'So. Why aren't you at the party?'

'I was at the party,' I say. 'I left. And came home.'

'Right. Was it no good?'

'It was fine,' I say. I read the next line of the instructions and pass the right screws over to Henry. 'It just wasn't really... I wanted to spend time with Dan, but it was packed and he was busy with his friends, so I just...'

'I get that,' Henry says. 'He didn't abandon you though?'

'No!' I say. Even though he did. A bit. 'No, he was great.'

And he was. And he was cool when I said I had to leave, even though I know he was getting really into the stuff we were doing on the bed 'cos I could feel his erection against my thigh.

On the way back on the Tube I wondered what sex with him would be like and I couldn't really picture it. Obviously I know what sex looks like, but when I tried to picture Dan slipping off my clothes, standing up and taking off his own, lying back down on top of me and actually going for it, I found that I just couldn't. Or maybe I didn't want to.

I don't know what that means. Or maybe I do.

'Where's Freya?' I ask Henry.

'With Georgie,' he says, frowning down at an electric screwdriver. 'How many of the two inch screws are left?'

I twist round until I find the right pile. 'Four.'

'Shit.' He sits back on his heels. 'We've gone wrong somewhere.'

*

Henry ends up having to undo all the screws he's put in so far and start the whole thing again. I get us both a beer. And then another. And by the time the bookcase is built, we're both a bit giddy. Henry's face is even pinker than when I came home and he's run his hands through his hair so many times that it's permanently on end. We both flop back onto the sofa.

'That,' I say, 'is a pretty perfect bookcase.'

Henry goes pinker. 'Yeah?' There's a bit at the base where we couldn't get the screws tight enough so some of the plain wood is showing, but that doesn't matter.

'Yeah. I love it. Thank you so much for buying it. And building it.'

'I have to admit,' he says. 'I thought it'd be easier.' He turns his hand over where a splinter is embedded in the soft flesh at the base of his thumb.

'You sure you don't want me to get that out for you?' I reach for his hand and pull it closer, peering at his thumb. There's a red spot with a dark dot.

'If you're still talking about sticking a needle in my hand, then yeah, I'm sure.'

'Wuss,' I say.

He grins. 'It'll work its way out on its own.'

'It will,' I tell him. 'Or you'll get septicaemia and die.'

'That's comforting. Thank you.'

And then I realise I'm basically holding his hand and I let go. He shifts on the sofa and then says, 'That's a good lookin' bookcase,' and holds his beer up to clink with mine.

We sit in silence for a while, both of us drinking our beer and smiling at the bookcase. I think about Anthony. About how I thought I was in love with him. I think about the dream, about how I was so sure that Dan was the man I was meant to be with. And I think about Henry, sitting next to me now, a possibly lethal shard of wood in his thumb from the bookcase he built for me. This is why I love romance novels and romcoms. Because real life is fucked all the way up. I finish my beer.

'How do you know when you're in love?' I ask Henry. I definitely shouldn't have another.

He makes a sound not dissimilar to 'Oof' and then says, 'Fuck, Bea, I don't know.'

'It's just…' I suddenly feel tearful and I'm not sure why. 'I've read all this stuff over the years and friends have told me, but I still don't know how anyone knows. You know, for sure.'

'I'm not sure anyone does for sure,' he says. 'You have to have faith.'

'I guess. I just wish I knew more about this stuff. I feel like… by my age, I should have more of a clue, you know?'

'I think everyone does,' he says. 'But for what it's worth, I think it's too soon for you to be talking about being in love with Dan.'

'Oh god, I know!' I say, and drink some more beer, before realising I finished mine and I've just taken his. 'It's just… it's not a normal situation. Like I know he's meant for me. I thought he was meant for me. It just doesn't—' I jump as the front door slams downstairs.

'Doesn't what?' Henry asks, looking at me intently.

Footsteps thunder up the stairs.

'Is Celine here?' Adam almost yells from the doorway.

'I don't think so,' I say, half-turning. 'What's wrong?'

'Fuck,' Adam says. He clambers over the back of the sofa and drops down next to me. 'I think she might've left me.'

'What happened?' I ask him, glancing at Henry. Celine still hasn't told him. I can't believe she still hasn't told him.

'She's just…' He rubs both hands over his face. 'She's not herself. And she won't tell me what's wrong. And everything I do and say seems to piss her off. And she said she'd had enough and she left and I thought she just meant she was going out for the evening, but she's not back and I think… I think this might be it. Fuck.'

'Have you called her?' Henry asks.

'Called. Texted. WhatsApped. All that bollocks. I don't know what the fuck I'm doing. Maybe she's right. Maybe we shouldn't be together. Should it be this hard? I don't know if it should be this hard.' He's more stressed than I've ever seen him before.

'I think,' Henry says. 'Maybe it has to be at least a bit hard, or it's not worth it, you know?'

Adam's hunched over, staring at the floor. 'That's what she said,' he says, morosely. He looks up. 'Fuck this. Have we got beer?'

Henry's leaning back on the sofa, staring up at the ceiling.

'Fridge,' he says.

*

When Adam gets back with beers for all three of us, he and Henry spend some time comparing relationships: Adam's first girlfriend who dumped him for his best friend and broke his heart; a girl at uni who wouldn't tell her friends about him, and made him pretend to be her personal trainer; an older woman he met on the bus and was really into until he found out she was married. Henry hasn't contributed much, but Adam doesn't seem to notice.

'What about you?' he asks me, eventually. 'Best and worst relationships?'

'That's easy,' I say.

'Aw, crap, I need a wazz,' Adam says and clambers over the sofa and out of the room.

I've only had a couple of beers. Plus the beers at Dan's, but I don't think they count since the Tube journey home must have negated any affect. But I feel loose and sleepy and buzzy at the same time. If I was a different kind of person, now's the time I'd say something like 'Let's go out!' and go and get dressed up and find a club and dance and go straight to work. I've never been that kind of person. Plus it's a Tuesday.

'Bea?' Henry says and I wonder if I've fallen asleep. I shuffle up the sofa, but it's too hard to hold my head up so I slide down again.

'That's easy,' I say again, even though Adam's not here any more. 'I've only had one relationship.'

'What?' Henry says.

'One relationship,' I repeat, enunciating clearly. Then I laugh. Maybe I'm a little drunk. 'And I'm not sure you can even call it a relationship really. Because it was rubbish. And then he disappeared.'

'Disappeared?'

I think Henry has shifted round so he's looking at me, but I don't want to turn and see his face. I close my eyes instead.

'Not, like, became invisible,' I say and then I sit up straight. 'Unless he did. That would explain it. But that's probably not what actually happened.' I flop back again.

'I wouldn't have thought so, no,' Henry says. 'But… how?'

I sigh. 'I don't know. Before him – Anthony – it just didn't happen. And then since him…' I wave my hands and hope I manage to convey all the things I can't possibly say and don't even usually allow myself to feel. It's a tall order, I know. But you can do it, hand!

'But you're…' Henry says.

I feel the sofa move next to me and I think he's leaning over to pick up his drink. He sits back up. I think.

'You're great,' he finishes.

I open my eyes and he's right in front of me. He looks startled and jerks his head back a little, but he doesn't move, he carries on looking. Into my eyes. My stomach lurches and for a second I think I might be sick, but it settles down into butterflies. Big, violent butterflies, but butterflies all the same. Flappy little bastards.

I glance down at Henry's mouth. He's got a nice mouth. I'm not sure I've thought about it before, but now, seeing it up close, I don't know how I missed it. Good lips. They look soft. I shouldn't be staring at his mouth. I look up at his eyes and he's still looking at me, a tiny line between his eyebrows.

'Bea—'

'Not interrupting anything, am I?' Adam bellows from behind my head.

I jump – why he can never just speak I don't know – and I see disappointment flash over Henry's face.

'No!' I say, but it comes out barely audibly.

Henry twists round so he's sitting next to me again and Adam sits on the back of the sofa and lets himself fall onto it so he's upside down next to me. He butts my knee with his head like a goat.

'Didn't even spill a drop!'

He holds a beer out to Henry and then me, before awkwardly shuffling himself round to sitting, kicking the door jamb as he does.

'Oi,' Henry says, mildly.

'Sorry, boss.'

I pull my legs up so I'm sitting cross-legged.

'What'd I miss?' Adam says. 'Thought I might come back to find you two making sweet, sweet love.'

'Fucking HELL,' Henry says at the same time as I say, 'What the fuck?'

'Sorry,' Adam says, holding his hands – one of them gripping his beer – up. 'I just always thought you two would be good together.'

Before either Henry or I can say anything, Adam groans dramatically and says, 'I would fucking kill for a cig.'

'You don't smoke,' Henry says.

'I used to,' Adam says. 'And I bloody loved it. Beer and a cig and, like, a curry? Best ever.'

'I could go for a curry,' I say. I didn't actually eat anything at Dan's party – which seems like ages ago now, even though it's not that late really – and I hadn't realised quite how hungry I was.

'I'll get it,' Adam says. 'Bhuna?'

'For you,' I say. 'I'll have… I don't know, dhansak?'

'I'm all right,' Henry says. 'I think I'll go to bed.'

I turn to look at him then and catch him looking at me.

'Don't,' I say. 'Stay up and have a curry.'

'And a cig,' Adam adds. 'Or. I could go and get some weed.' He scrambles to his feet and starts checking his pockets for, presumably, his phone and wallet.

'Yes to curry, no to weed,' Henry says.

'Yeah,' Adam says. 'Live a little.'

'We have to be up in eight hours,' Henry tells me.

I shrug. 'I've never stayed up all night. And I've never done weed.'

'What?!' Adam says, outraged. 'Jesus, Bea, you really haven't lived.' He climbs over the sofa again and says, 'Won't be long.'

'I know,' I say, but he's already gone.

Henry stares at me for a second and I can't quite figure out the expression on his face. He looks confused and also fond, but something else. I look down at my beer. When did I get another beer?

The door slams downstairs.

'He probably won't come back,' Henry says. 'He'll end up going to a club or getting arrested.'

'Or Celine will come back and then we'll be stuck here, listening to them.'

My face heats at the idea of sitting here with Henry while Adam and Celine are making their sex noises.

'I once heard him shout, "Not in there!"' Henry says. 'I had to knock myself out with a brick.'

I snort with laughter. 'Oh my god. I mean, it's nice that they've got each other.'

'There's a lid for every pot, my nan used to say.'

I smile. 'Do you believe that?'

Henry frowns. 'I think... maybe? Sort of? I don't think I believe in soulmates or The One or anything like that. But I think it means you find the one that fits you best. And it might not be exactly right – maybe it's a bit cracked or bent or the handle's missing or you're a red pot and the lid's blue or it's not even a proper lid, maybe it's a plate? But they fit together anyway. Do you know what I mean?'

I nod. 'Yeah. I think that's what I believe too. Maybe.'

'Yeah? 'Cos I thought you were looking for the man of your dreams. I thought you'd found him.'

I'm startled to find my eyes fill with tears. 'I don't know. It's so strange 'cos I spent so long waiting to find him. I was so sure that's what the dream meant. And... in the dream it felt so right, you know? I know it's mad. I do.' I drink. 'I'm just not sure now.'

'About Dan?'

'Mm.' I drink some more. Even though I know I should stop. I should've stopped a while ago.

'But it's early days,' Henry says. 'You've only been out, what? Twice? You hardly even know him.'

'Four times,' I say. 'Five including tonight. But you're right.'

But I know enough to know it's not right – it doesn't feel like I want it to feel. And I really don't know what to do with that information.

CHAPTER TWENTY-EIGHT

'What's that?' I ask Adam. He wasn't gone long at all and now he's resting something on a copy of *Men's Health* magazine and poking it with a knife.

'Seriously?' He glances up at me. 'Jesus, Bea.'

'Is that weed?' I look at Henry to see if Adam's taking the piss, but Henry nods at me. 'It looks like an Oxo cube.'

'It's resin. I can't believe you've never even seen it before,' Adam says, taking out a packet of Rizlas.

'I've seen, like, joints.' I don't tell him I've only seen them in films. 'But not like that.'

I watch him roll it and then he hands it to me. 'OK, so just breathe it in slowly. Don't take a massive drag 'cos it'll hit the back of your throat and make you cough.'

I take the joint from him and put it to my lips. I take the tiniest, most tentative drag and hand it to Henry.

'You're all right,' Henry says.

'Henry.' Adam looks up. 'My relationship is over. You have to share my misery. Plus Beanie Baby's never done this before, so we have to show her the ways.'

'Jesus, OK,' Henry says.

I say, 'Beanie Baby?'

Adam grins at me. 'And get the fuck on with it. The curry's going cold.'

I take another drag. The curry smells really good. The weed not so much.

'Try to hold it a bit longer this time,' Adam says.

I do. Not much longer, but a bit.

'I can't feel anything,' I say, after a couple more goes. 'It's not working.'

'Just wait,' Adam tells me. 'It will.'

Adam bought way too much curry. It feels like we're taking cardboard lids off foil cartons forever. I fold a poppadom into my mouth and laugh at the crunch it makes.

'You're wasted,' Adam says, pointing at me.

He looks a bit blurry.

'Takes one to know one,' I say.

Or maybe it's my eyes.

He hoots. 'So wasted.'

I'm piling chicken tikka masala onto rice and marvelling at the colour – it looks like rubies, like mushed rubies, or something else… lava! – when I hear someone coming up the stairs.

'Freya!' I shout. 'Come and have some curry and weeeeeeed.'

But it's not Freya. It's Celine.

'Oh fucking hell, babe.' Adam launches himself over the sofa and grabs Celine by the shoulders. 'I thought you'd left me.'

'You seem really cut up about it,' she says. 'Can you move this? I need to sit down.'

Adam shoves the sofa out of the way and Celine walks around it and then sits down heavily.

'Where've you been?' He holds a joint out to her and she waves it away.

'To see Mum.' She tips her head back and closes her eyes. 'God that smells amazing. Can I have some?'

'Your mum?' Adam says, as I pass Celine a naan and one of the foil pots. A greeny one.

'Yeah. She gave me money for a cab. I was going to leave earlier, but she was freaking out about her neighbour's greenhouse or something. I stopped listening.'

'Why?'

'Oh I don't know, something to do with growing tomatoes.'

'No,' Adam says. 'Why did you go and see your mum?'

'Oh.' Celine sits up and looks at him. 'Because I'm pregnant.'

Silence. I look at Henry and he's already looking back at me, his eyebrows halfway to his hairline.

And then Adam whoops. He jumps up and swings round wildly, looking from me to Henry and then back to Celine.

'Are you fucking serious?'

'Well, I'm not fucking joking.'

Celine sounds like herself, but she looks nervous. She's picking at one of her nails, and she's paler than usual. Although that could be the puking.

'Oh my god,' Adam says. 'Oh my god. I thought you'd left me.'

Celine laughs and pushes one of her hands into his short hair. 'As. If.'

They stare at each other just long enough that I start to feel uncomfortable and then Adam grabs her. I watch her face over his shoulder. She's got her eyes closed, but she just looks blissfully happy. I eat another poppadom.

Adam leans back, holding her at arms' length. He was kneeling to hug her, but now he plants one foot on the floor, pushes himself up on one knee, and says, 'Celine. I love you. And I love our baby. Will you marry me?'

I look at Henry. His hand, holding a chunk of naan, has stopped halfway to his open mouth. He looks as stunned as I feel.

Celine laughs. 'No! I told you. Well. Not yet. But yes. Eventually. Obviously.'

'That's good enough for me!' Adam yells. He stands up, leans over, and lifts her bodily off the couch.

'Night, you two,' he says over his shoulder as he carries his girlfriend out of the room. 'Don't do anything we wouldn't do.'

✴

'God,' Henry says, once they've gone.

'I know,' I say. I do feel a bit wasted now, but it might be tiredness. Or just how surreal that was.

'It just shows,' Henry says. 'You can never really know about someone else's relationship.'

'I think they're going to be OK,' I say. 'I hope so.'

'A baby Adam or Celine,' Henry says.

I snort with laughter. 'What a frightening thought.'

'Cool though.'

'Very cool.'

We sit in silence for a little while and I pick at the curry. I am still so bloody hungry. Oh. I bet that's the weed.

'So,' Henry says.

I look over at him. He's leaning back against the sofa and at some point he's taken his hoodie off and he's wearing a white T-shirt with a baggy neck and a couple of little holes near the hem.

'I think moths have been at your shirt,' I tell him, squinting to see it more clearly. I glimpse a bit of his skin through the holes and stop squinting, my cheeks heating.

He stretches the shirt out to look at the holes and accidentally reveals a strip of belly. It looks soft. But there's definition too, not a six pack, but those vertical lines. And another line. Of hair. That disappears under behind the waistband of his trackie bottoms. I blow out a breath and pick up another piece of naan, dragging it through the curry, and then folding it into my mouth.

'I've had this for years,' Henry says. 'It's knackered, but it's soft and comfy and it reminds me of home.'

I smile, covering my hand with my mouth 'cos curry. 'That's cute.'

'It was hard to be away from home,' he says. 'When I first moved here. So I ended up clinging to a lot of stuff.' He shrugs. 'Actually, that should have been my most embarrassing thing no one knows. I basically wear a blankie in bed.'

'You sleep in it?' I say. 'I wondered about that. 'Cos you always get dressed before you come out of your room.'

He shakes his head, fiddling with the holey bit of the shirt. 'No. I sleep naked. But I wear it round the house – not usually on its own though.'

I shove more naan in my mouth. My brain is stuck on 'I sleep naked'. All the times I've wondered about Henry – when Adam's been in his tiny pants or shorts, Celine in one of Adam's football shirts or her Slytherin pyjama bottoms, Freya in her transparent vests and lacy knickers – I always pictured him in proper pyjamas. With buttons. Sometimes with a belted dressing gown over the top. I never imagined he'd sleep naked.

My mouth's dry. I reach for the nearest beer and take a long gulp. I really shouldn't have any more beer.

'Were you lonely?' Henry asks. 'When you moved here?'

I gulp some more. 'A bit,' I say. 'In Acton, definitely. But then I met you. Got the job, I mean. And moved in here. And then it was better.'

'Why did you want to move here?' he asks. He pulls his leg up and his bare foot brushes against my thigh. I glance at it. He's got nice feet, Henry. I'm not a fan of feet in general – Adam's are gross, his toenails actually curl under his toes, and he lost one when he did a marathon and it never grew back – but Henry's are nice: smooth and tan and not hairy.

I eat more naan and wonder whether I should tell him. The real reason. Not the reason I usually give people. But then he has just told me he wears a blankie. I swallow.

'Because of the dream,' I say before I can change my mind. 'Not to London – I wanted to move to London anyway – but to this part of London. Here. That's why I moved here.'

Henry nods. He doesn't look appalled or disappointed or like he's thinking of jumping up and running away. 'I figured,' he says.

'What?'

He shrugs. 'You used to go and hang around in the park all the time. Waiting for him to turn up. I didn't think of it straight away, but eventually I realised that was why. To make it easier to find him.'

I nod. 'Right.'

'And now you've found him.'

I blink. Henry is looking at me sort of intensely. There's a small frown line between his eyebrows and he's staring and staring. I want to make a joke, take the piss, but I can't.

'And now I've found him,' I agree.

CHAPTER TWENTY-NINE

I'm in the park. The sun's shining and the leaves are fluttering over my head and casting shadows on the path in front of me. I see Dan in the distance, but he's not walking towards me, he's walking towards the park gates.

I shout his name, but no sound comes out. I try to run to catch up with him, but my legs don't move at all. A flock of pigeons appear and block my view. Once they're gone, I look for Dan, but I can't see him. He's disappeared.

And then I wake up.

✢

'Can you come home?' Matt says, as soon as I answer my phone.

My stomach drops. 'What's happened? What's wrong?'

'I don't want to tell you on the phone. Just… can you come? Today?'

'You have to tell me, you can't leave it like that.'

I feel like I can hear him thinking. 'Right. OK. I'm sorry. Tom did it. He's been stealing from the business. For years. Mum might lose the house.'

I can't breathe. There are dots in front of my eyes and I can't breathe. I feel a hand on my arm and I know it's Henry. He guides me towards the staff room and then I'm sitting down.

'Bea?' Matt says, in my ear.

'I'm OK,' I tell him, even though of course I'm not. 'How's Mum?'

'Devastated. She's thrown him out. Can you come?'

I can't even think. 'I'm at work.'

'It's fine,' Henry says. He's got his back to me and I realise he's making tea.

'I can come,' I tell Matt.

He's already Googled the train times, so he tells me and I repeat them so Henry can write them down on the kitchen rota on the wall. There's a pen attached with string to encourage people to fill it in.

'Where's Tom?' I ask Matt.

'I don't know. I haven't seen him. He was already gone when I got here.'

'Fuck,' I breathe.

'I know. Text me when you get to Stockport and I'll come and pick you up.'

I hang up the phone and Henry turns and hands me a cup of tea.

'I need to go,' I tell him.

'Just stay there for a minute. I'm going to close the shop.'

'You can't,' I say, but he's already gone. If a secret shopper turns up and the shop's closed during business hours, Henry will get fired. But I guess that's unlikely. I press a hand against my stomach and for a second I think I might be sick, but no. I breathe in the steam from the tea, blowing over the surface. I can smell the sugar.

'You OK?' Henry says, coming back and leaning against the units.

'How many sugars did you put in?'

'Three. That's what they say, don't they? For shock?'

'I think so.' I sip tentatively, but it's still too hot. 'Tom's been stealing from the business. Mum's thrown him out. And she might lose the house.' I can't believe I'm even saying it. It doesn't seem real.

'I'm so sorry.'

'I can't believe it. All this time. Poor Mum.' I can't even think about Tom. I can't even think about how he's lied to us all this time.

'Do you want me to come with you?' Henry asks.

I look up at him. His hair's all tufty where he's run his hand through it. His glasses are smudged. His cheeks are pink and he's biting at his lip. Something flutters in my chest, but I shove it away.

'No. Thank you. That's really lovely of you. But I'm fine.'

I drink some tea. It's ridiculously sweet. But good.

'There's a train every twenty minutes,' Henry says. 'Finish that and then I'll walk you to the station. Or home. To get your stuff.'

I don't want to go home. I just want to get on the train and go. I've got my bag. I've got clothes at Mum's. I can buy a toothbrush at the station. I just want to go.

'Honestly, I'm fine. You don't need to do that. And you should go and open up again. I'll drink this and then I'll go. I don't want you to get in trouble.'

'You're shaking,' he says, reaching out and catching my fingers with his. He only leaves them for a second and then he pulls away. I'm scared to look up at him.

'I'll be fine once I've had this.'

'OK,' he says. 'But I'm not opening up. I'm staying here. Unless you want me to go?'

'No,' I say, finally looking up and smiling weakly at him. 'You're fine.'

While I drink the tea, all I can think about it how Tom came into our lives and made us all feel so much more secure. He fitted right in. He made us laugh. There was always so much love in our house and Tom was a big part of that. I can't bear to think that any of it wasn't real. I can't bear to know he's done this to Mum. To all of us.

✻

'Will you be OK on your own?' I ask Henry as I leave a few minutes later.

It's only when I see him smile that I realise what I've said. I meant it. I wasn't joking.

'I'll manage,' he says.

I nod, my hand on the door.

'Ring me when you get there,' he says. 'Or text or whatever. WhatsApp. Not right away, obviously, I know your mum… But I mean, just let me know.'

I nod. 'I will. And you'll tell the others?'

'Course.'

I pull the door open and I'm about to step through it, the bell still jangling above my head, when I feel Henry's hand on my arm and I turn back. He grabs my other arm and pulls me towards him and I go easily, relaxing against his chest, my arms sliding around his waist. I breathe him in: his face resting on the top of my head, my face against his shoulder, his arms around my back. He's always given good hugs, but I don't think I've ever had one quite like this before. I pull away when I feel myself starting to tear up.

'It'll be OK,' he says against my hair.

I nod. 'Thank you.'

And then I leave.

✻

The house looks the same as always. There's a new cat bed, and a fresh coat of paint in the porch, but apart from that everything's the same. But it feels different. Usually when I come home, Tom picks me up at the station and on the short journey home gives me all the local gossip. He's in the Rotary Club and does the Parkrun every Saturday morning and spends every Sunday evening in the White Lion on the green. He knows everything. Knew. I guess I have to start thinking of him in the past tense.

'Tea?' Matt says, as I follow him into the kitchen.

'I'll make it. You make horrible tea. Where's Mum?'

He fills the kettle. 'Garden.'

I pass him and go through the conservatory and down the steps to the garden. At first I can't see her, but then I spot her sitting on the bench under the tree in the far corner. I cross the lawn, stepping on the stones Tom laid just after they bought this house, and sit down next to her, dropping my head down on her shoulder.

'Hello, darling,' she says, leaning her head against mine.

'I'm so sorry, Mum.'

She sighs. 'I can't believe I've been so stupid.'

I sit up straight. 'How were you supposed to know? Phil didn't even know.'

Phil was Tom's business partner for twenty years. He was the one who reported him. He'd suspected for quite some time, conducted a bit of an investigation of his own, and then approached Tom with it. But Tom completely denied it. And then Phil had no choice but to report it.

'He's devastated. They've been friends for so long. He can't believe Tom's done this. I can't believe he's done this.'

'Me neither,' I say.

I couldn't stop thinking about it on the train. That it must be a mistake. That Tom would never do anything dishonest, never do anything to risk his and Mum's home. He's always been so good. To all of us. From the first time we met him. He's always been warm and wise and safe and secure and funny and kind. How can that not be real? And how can he not be in our family any more?

'Have you spoken to him?' I ask Mum.

'Phil? A bit, I—'

'No. Not Phil. Tom.'

'Oh.' She sighs. 'No. He's texted me. And he sent flowers, ridiculously. I don't have anything more to say to him, to be honest.'

'So what happens now? Matt said something about the house?'

As if I've conjured him up, Matt comes out of the house and walks down the steps, holding a tray of mugs that rattle as he walks.

'Oh god,' Mum says. 'Did he make tea? He makes bloody horrible tea.'

I laugh for the first time in hours. 'I said that to him. I was going to do it.'

The three of us sit in the garden, drinking our tea and watching birds fly in and out of the hedge.

'I can't believe there's so many,' I say at one point. Or that they fly across the garden so quickly and just smash right into the hedge, like they're ram-raiding it.

'It's 'cos of Tom's fat balls,' Mum says and then snorts with laughter. 'Oh god.' She puts her hands up to her face and I press up against her side.

'That's one of the worst things,' she sniffles from behind her hands. 'Already. We've got so many bloody in-jokes. And now they're all gone. I've lost it all. I can't believe I'm crying about his stupid fat balls.'

She wipes her face, sits up straight, and drinks some tea. 'I'm sorry. I keep crying at the most ridiculous things.'

'It's fine,' I say, rubbing her arm. I have no idea what to say, no idea what I can do to make her feel better. But there isn't anything I can do, is there? How could there be?

CHAPTER THIRTY

The following morning, Mum wakes me with a cup of tea and a slice of toast, thick with butter. I groan, covering my eyes with my arm. We drank a lot of wine last night. A lot.

'I need to go into work,' Mum says, perched on the edge of my bed. 'Come with me? Matt's going to see Kevin.'

Kevin was his best mate at school and is now deputy head of the same school. I had a crush on him all through school, but haven't stalked him on Facebook for ages now.

'How are you so perky?' I ask Mum. 'My head is killing me.'

'Drank a pint of water before bed,' she says. 'And I've just had about four espressos. We need to go before I start stripping the walls or dismantling the furniture.'

'Ugh.' I drag myself to sitting and force my eyes open.

Not only is she perky, she looks amazing. Her long dark hair is thick and shiny and her eyes are bright. I don't think she's wearing eye make-up behind her glasses, but her eyebrows are done and her lips shine with bright red gloss. Sickening.

'I'll give you fifteen to come round, then you have to get in the shower. I'll have another brew waiting for you downstairs. Do you want an espresso? Tom—' She stops, closes her eyes and shakes her head. 'Tom made me buy one of those coffee machines. With the pods. It's actually very good.'

I reach over and squeeze her hand. She's still wearing all her rings: engagement, wedding, eternity.

'I'll be down in a bit, OK?'

She leans over and kisses me on the forehead, then wipes any trace of lipstick away with her thumb. She smells the same as she has for as long as I can remember: Estée Lauder Youth Dew. When I first moved to London, I used to sometimes go into department stores and spray a bit on my wrist. It doesn't suit me at all, but I loved feeling like she was there with me.

Once she's gone, I swing my legs out of bed and stretch my neck from side to side, listening to it crack and pop. I stand up, tentatively, and then sit down again. I think I'd better drink my tea first. I drink it while I scroll through my phone. There are a few WhatsApp messages from Freya and Henry, checking in with me, saying they hope everything's OK, and one from Celine saying *Worried I might puke up a lung. When you come home can you smother me with a pillow?*

Once I've finished my tea, I stagger from the bed to the bathroom and the shower does actually make me feel a lot better. At least hangover-wise. There are so many reminders of Tom everywhere that it's impossible to not think about him for long. His shaving cream is still on the window ledge; his and Mum's wedding photo is framed on the landing. I stare at it for a while – they both look so happy. We were so happy. Was he stealing and lying even back then?

*

Mum's shop is inside a Victorian arcade off the main street. It's beautiful: black and white tile floor, polished wood fittings and benches and a glass roof. It's quiet at this time of the day, but classical music is playing, and it feels like an oasis of calm.

Mum unlocks the shop and I follow her in. When I lived here, this shop was a high end jeweller's and I never went inside, only glanced through the window, and it's completely different now. Each side of the shop is lined with clothing. Too much to take in straight away – all I'm aware of is velvet and lace and sequins and so much colour. There are carousels of more clothes down the centre of the shop and chandeliers overhead, that Mum switches on from just inside the door. They're not too bright; they infuse the shop with a warm glow.

'Tea?' Mum says, half-turning to me.

I'm still looking around, my mouth hanging open.

'This is so beautiful,' I say.

She beams at me over her shoulder. 'Isn't it? I love it. Lucy's off today, which is a shame. I wanted her to meet you. I've told her all about you.'

Lucy is the owner. She and Mum used to work together years ago and have always kept in touch.

'She bought this place after her divorce.'

I follow Mum towards the back of the shop.

'I guess I need to talk to her now. She can give me even more advice than she has already.'

'So you're definitely doing... that?' I ask, stopping with my hands on the polished wooden desk.

Mum turns and her face has fallen.

'I'm sorry, darling. That was glib.'

'No,' I say. 'It's OK.' I know that she always makes light of the things that hurt her the most. She always has.

'I'll make us tea and then we can talk,' she says, walking further into the back of the shop. 'Have a look around.'

While Mum makes tea, I weave between the carousels, just touching fabrics and trying to take everything in. There's a flowered yellow tea dress that I immediately picture myself wearing with my brown suede boots and denim jacket. I spot a rail of bags and nip straight over to look at a beaded shell clutch. I open it and run my fingers over the satin lining. Everything in here is beautiful. In fact, the whole shop is so beautiful it doesn't even seem real. It's like something from a film. It feels like a place where magical things will happen. Like someone could step into the changing room and come out a completely different person.

※

'I know it's hard to take in,' Mum says, once she's made the tea and we're sitting on a curvy velvet sofa at the back of the shop. 'But this level of… betrayal…' She shakes her head. 'I could never trust him again.'

'I know,' I say. 'I mean, I understand that.'

'I love him.' Her eyes fill and she shakes her head. 'I probably always will. But there's no way I could ever get over this. And he knows. He understands. I think.'

I realise I'm fiddling with a loose thread on the arm of the sofa and make myself stop – I don't want to unravel the whole thing.

'Did he say why he did it? Like… was he in trouble? To begin with?' This is the one thing I've been consoling myself with, that maybe he was forced into it somehow, that he didn't choose it.

Mum sighs. 'I think originally he did actually take some to pay an unexpected bill. His divorce from Janine. I think. But that's absolutely no reason to keep doing it. I think he kept doing it because it was easy. And he didn't get caught. He said he always intended to pay it back and it just got away from him, but frankly that's absolute bollocks.' She drinks some tea. 'He did it because he could.'

A customer comes in and Mum goes off to help them, while I finish my tea and think about Tom. He was always, for me, the perfect example of what a man could and should be. He was warm and funny and generous. He supported and cared for Mum and me and Matt, pretty much from the moment we met him. And while I don't believe his love for her or for us was a lie, it blows my mind that he could be so great in so many ways, but at the same time let us all down so badly in so many others. Particularly Mum. I worry that if it was me I would accept his apology. I would forgive him. Like I forgave Anthony so many times when he didn't treat me well at all. Like I accepted that Dan's 'test' was a reasonable thing for him to do. Mum is stronger than me. She always has been, she's had to be. But that's no reason for me to accept being treated badly.

'Tell me about Dan,' Mum says, once she's finished with the customer and is sitting next to me again.

I shake my head. 'I was just thinking about him.'

'Oh,' she says, dipping her head to look at my face. 'That's not a happy face.'

And I start to cry.

*

I tell her everything. I tell her about the dream, that it's the reason I moved to London, the reason I live where I live. I tell her about meeting him in the park. I tell her about how the dreams have changed since I met him. I tell her about Anthony and how he treated me like shit. I tell her about the party and Dan's test. And I tell her that all this time I've wanted what she and Tom had and now I don't know what to do. By the time I'm finished, we're both a snotty mess and it's lucky that part-way through the conversation she turned the sign on the door to 'closed'.

'My love,' she says, once she's made us another cup of tea and we've dried our tears and blown our noses. 'I don't know where you got the idea that you are not entirely perfect as you are. I hope it wasn't from me.'

I shake my head. 'No. You've always been—'

She holds her hand up to stop me. 'I think, I hope, our house was always full of love.'

'It was,' I say. 'It still is.'

'And we always loved you no matter what. Tom too. Don't forget that. As angry as I am with him, as much as our marriage is over, he'll always be in my life and he should always be in yours too.'

I nod. I have been thinking about that. I'm not ready to see him yet, but I will be one day. I hope.

'I understand why the dream was important to you,' she says, reaching for my hand. 'That feeling of warmth, of security, of being wholly loved…' She shakes her head. 'I get it. But it sounds like you've used the dream to kind of insulate you against a real relationship. Because real relationships are hard and messy and often disappointing. And sometimes they end. And that has to be OK. Because if you're avoiding all of that, you don't have a real relationship.'

I'm crying again. I squeeze her fingers so she knows I get it.

'Dan sounds great. Although I'm not keen on the "test" business. But he's not the one for you. You know that. And maybe there is no "one" for you. Maybe you're the one for you.' She lifts my chin with her index finger. 'You know that, right?'

I'm working on it.

*

'Look at this,' Mum says later, after she's reopened the shop, and we've had quite a few customers. I've watched Mum with them and she's amazing. She seems to know what they want and exactly what will work for them within just a few seconds. I've been in awe, watching her.

Right now she's holding out an absolutely glorious dress. It's just a simple shift shape, but it's beaded and sequinned all over. It's silver and the top has a scalloped pattern, while the bottom half has grey stripes crossing over and edged with what look like pearls.

'Gorgeous,' I say, reaching out to run my fingers over the fabric.

'Try it on,' she says.

I shake my head. 'I'd never wear it.'

'You don't know,' she says. 'Just try it on. I think it'll look beautiful on you.'

The changing room is behind a thick velvet curtain and is as glamorous as the rest of the shop, with a huge mirror with a wide gold frame, fairy lights, another chandelier and a velvet covered curvy chair. I pull off my leggings and hoodie and fold them on the chair, then I take the dress off the hanger.

It's surprisingly heavy and feels cool to the touch. I drop it over my head and it shimmers itself down my body. And then I stare at myself in the mirror. It looks amazing. I think. It's a perfect fit and looks like it's made for me. It makes my skin look better, my eyes brighter, my hair thicker. It's a magic dress. I want to take a photo on my phone and send it to everyone I know. I turn around to look at the back and then I do take a photo and I send it to Freya.

'Have you got it on?' Mum says from the other side of the curtain. Let's see.'

I pull back the curtain.

'Oh!' Mum says, clasping her hands under her chin and beaming at me. 'Right. Well.' She clears her throat and I can see her eyes are shining with tears. My eyes immediately fill too. 'So you're definitely having that,' she says.

※

I've been in bed for what feels like hours, but I'm still not asleep. I've tried reading, watching my favourite bit of *You've Got Mail* ('I hoped it was you') on my phone, even a few of my favourite daydreams (fantasies, I think I should call them now. Fantasies), but I still feel wide awake. One of the things that bugs me in a lot of the romance novels I read is that the main character has no agency. Things just happen to her and she lets them. She doesn't do anything to change them. Her father throws her out of the house and she doesn't argue, she leaves, and then she meets someone, often a woman her own age, but with a much stronger personality, and lives with them until she meets the man. The one. And he saves her. And I love that. I do. But sometimes I wish these women would just save themselves. Or save the man even. Men must need saving sometimes, I'm sure they must.

But I've been doing the same thing. Yes, I chose to leave home, but I picked a place to live based on a dream. A dream! Mum's right. That's ridiculous. I guess I could argue that I am responsible for the dream because I dreamt it. It was my dream. It came from my subconscious. But. But I wouldn't be going out with Dan if it wasn't for the dream. We don't have anything in common. I don't even really fancy him. I don't feel anything when he kisses me. I really don't. So what am I doing? Am I just going to keep going out with him because I dreamt about it? Or am I going to actually think about what I want and go after that?

I need to end things with Dan. I know I do. I don't know how to do that. I've never had a break-up, since Anthony just disappeared, but I'm sure Freya will tell me. And she'll be delighted.

I roll over, punching my pillow. I don't know what I want. But I know it's not Dan. But if I don't have the dream, if I don't have that hope that everything will be OK, that there is someone for me and I just have to find them, then I don't know where to start. Does that mean I should stop trying to find someone who makes me feel the way the dream makes me feel? Or does it mean he's still out there, he's just not Dan? If Dan isn't the man of my dreams, does that mean the dream wasn't real? If Tom can screw Mum over does that mean there's no such thing as a dream relationship? No such thing as The One?

But I can't let myself believe that. I've wanted it for so long. Ten years. I planned my life around it. If I don't have that, what do I have?

CHAPTER THIRTY-ONE

I'm in the park. The sun's shining, but it's raining too. I look up and, over the Greek coffee shop, a rainbow is curving, the colours sharp and bright.

I walk further into the park, looking for Dan on the bench, Anthony on the bandstand, pigeons anywhere, but there's no one here. I'm alone. And I feel fine. I'm not scared or nervous or anxious. I feel relaxed, warmed by the sun.

I sit down on one of the deckchairs and close my eyes, the sun warming my face. Music starts to play and at first I can't place it, but eventually I recognise it and I smile. 'It Had to be You'.

And then I wake up.

*

'Henry phoned,' Mum says when I get downstairs in the morning. 'He said he didn't want to try your mobile in case you were asleep.'

'Is everything OK?' I ask, sitting down at the dining table. I sit in my usual seat on the left hand side because Tom always sits at the head and Mum next to him, opposite me. Sat. Tom always sat.

'Think so. He didn't say otherwise. I think he just wanted to know you were OK. Or when you were coming home. He's such a sweetheart.'

'He is,' I say.

I pour myself a tea from the pot on the table. Mum's making a cooked breakfast and the smell makes my mouth water and my stomach rumble.

Matt comes in, scratching his belly under his T-shirt, his hair standing on end. He sits next to me and I pour him a tea too.

'My bed here is so much comfier than home,' he says. 'Our mattress is shit.'

'You should buy a better one,' Mum says, checking on the bacon under the grill. 'A good night's sleep is so important.'

'Lydia likes it,' Matt says. 'It's so hard, I might as well be sleeping on the floor.'

'How is Lydia?' I ask.

He shrugs. 'Same. Busy. She wants a baby.'

Mum drops the spatula she's holding and says, 'Oh shitsticks.'

I grin at Matt.

'She's not pregnant, Mother,' he says. 'We've just been talking about it.'

Mum's running the spatula under the tap. 'I'm too young to be a nan.'

'You're not actually,' Matt says, and then ducks when she throws a tea towel at him. 'But… I don't know. I'm not sure. Not yet anyway.'

'Not sure you want a baby?' I ask him.

'Not sure I want one with Lydia,' he says, rubbing his face.

Oh. Shit.

*

On the train home, I think about Mum and Tom and me and Dan, and Matt and Lydia. I have to admit that I never knew what he saw in her in the first place – she always seemed cold and unfriendly to me – but I thought he liked that. I thought he liked her bossiness and efficiency and organisation skills and I think he did, at first. But he said that now he feels more like an employee than a husband. And that they never even laugh together any more. Mum said that was particularly important – that even when she and Tom had rough times before, they'd always been able to

Keris Stainton

laugh about it. So far, she hasn't been able to find the funny side
of the whole embezzlement thing.

It was so lovely being home that I want to make time to get
home more often. Plus Mum said she's definitely going to sell the
house – she wants to buy somewhere much smaller and, she says,
simplify her life. I get it. But it's going to be hard to say goodbye
to that house. So many of my happiest times took place there.

Matt says he's coming down to London for work next month
and we're going to go out for lunch. We're also going to try to
phone each other more often. I realised this weekend how much
I've missed him.

I spend much of the train journey reminiscing and feeling sad
about what we've lost as a family, what I've lost, what I thought
I had – or was going to have – that just wasn't real. But as the
train pulls into Euston – when I look out of the window and
see all the electric pylons, the tower blocks in the distance, the
graffiti on the sidings – I realise that the life I have is the life I
used to dream about.

Coming back to London still gives me a thrill. Every time.

                                   ❧

'We're taking you out to dinner,' Freya says when I get home. 'I
know you're probably tired, but we all want to do this, so tough tits.'

'That's very sweet of you,' I say, laughing. But it is. So I hug
her too.

'Missed you,' she says, into my hair. 'You OK?'

'Yeah. It was actually really lovely.'

'How's your mum?'

I don't get to tell her because Henry joins us in the kitchen
and immediately wraps his arms around both of us.

'Oof,' Freya says into my neck. 'All right, Henry, I know you've
been dying to get your hands on Bea, but what am I? Collateral
damage?'

Henry immediately lets go of both of us and crashes backwards into one of the units.

'Shit,' he says. 'Sorry.'

'I was only joking!' Freya says, but her voice sounds weird. Henry's gone bright red, which doesn't surprise me, but I think Freya might actually be blushing too. I've never seen her blush. It's weird.

'Gonna go and get changed,' Freya says and legs it. Huh.

'So was your mum OK?' Henry says. His face has calmed down a little but it's still pink. I think he's had his hair cut while I've been away. It's shorter round the ears. It suits him.

'Yeah. She's amazing. I went to work with her one day. The shop's great and she's really good. The customers love her.' I'm babbling. 'How was work?'

'Fine, yeah. I told head office you were away and they sent Craig in. So he was glad of the overtime.'

I nod. 'Good. Great. Yeah.' Oh god. 'Where are we going, do you know?'

He shakes his head. 'Oh, only the pub, I think. The Stag. But Adam's paying – did Freya tell you? He got a bonus.'

Adam works in IT consulting and none of us knows exactly what he does. But he earns really good money and every now and then he gets a bonus and takes us out for dinner. I haven't paid for a meal for days now, it must be the secret upside of your parents' marriage falling apart. Then again, I'm probably going to miss out on Christmas presents, so it will even out eventually.

*

It's another nice evening so we sit outside the pub. When we moved here, this place was rough. Me and Henry came in one night after work and conversation stopped, like something from a Western, while everyone checked us out. And then went back to their pool and darts and staring up at some foreign football

match on the TV above the bar. And then it closed for six months
and reopened as a gastropub. Henry was against it at first – he
said he liked the 'authenticity' of the original place. But then he
tried the steak and chips and it won him over.

The beer garden – or 'patio garden' as it is now – is lit with
multicoloured bulbs hanging from the trees and heated with an
open fire set into the wall. We pull two wooden tables together
and arrange our chairs around and Adam goes to the bar and
comes back with shots for everyone but Celine.

'Bloody typical,' she says, taking a small bottle of ginger ale
from the tray.

'So,' Adam says. 'Before we begin the festivities, Celine and I
have an announcement.'

'Celine's pregnant!' Freya says. 'Oh wait, we knew that.'

'You're getting married!' Henry laughs. 'No, we knew that
too…'

'Shut up, dickheads,' Adam says. 'We're moving to Southend.'

'No!' I say, before I can stop myself. Everyone looks at me. 'I
mean, I'm happy for you. If you're happy?' I look at Celine and
she nods. 'But I'll miss you so much.'

'It's time,' Celine says. 'I know I said I couldn't do it, but we
can hardly raise a baby in that one room.'

'Why have you stayed so long?' Freya asks them. 'You must've
been able to afford somewhere bigger for a while.'

Celine shrugs. 'It's fun. I love living with you lot.'

My eyes fill with tears and Adam bumps my shoulder with
his arm. 'It was only ever meant to be temporary. But we got
attached.'

I shake my head. It's way too early in the evening for me to
be crying in the pub.

'We did look into buying somewhere here,' Adam says. ''Cos
Cel wasn't sure about the whole family at the seaside thing—'

'But we looked at what we could get for our money here,' Celine interrupts. 'And what we can get there and... there's no contest. And you can all come and visit.'

'We definitely will,' Henry says.

'Of course we will,' Freya confirms.

I picture Celine and Adam and a baby in a big house by the sea. Everything's changing.

I pick up my glass of god-only-knows-what and hold it out to the others, who hold up their glasses too.

'To happy endings,' I say.

Adam snorts.

'And new beginnings,' Celine adds. We crash our glasses together.

CHAPTER THIRTY-TWO

'I'm sorry I didn't get a chance to look into that thing with your stepdad,' Dan says, once we've been seated.

We're in The Diner again. I wasn't sure about meeting here because it's where we had our first date, but it was easy enough for us both to get to and I knew it was nice and also it means I can leave and get the Tube and be home pretty swiftly. After.

'That's OK,' I tell him. Even though if he had looked into it, he could've given us a heads-up and we wouldn't have been blindsided. But then again, I'm not sure any of us would have believed it.

'I emailed a mate about it, but he didn't get back to me. He always was a bit of a shiftless git, to be honest.'

He's holding the menu up in front of his face and half of me is glad, while the other half wants to pull it down, say 'I'm sorry, this isn't working for me,' and do a runner.

'What are you having?' he says, smiling at me over the top of the menu.

God, this is awful. He's nice. He's actually really nice. I picked him up in a park because I thought I saw him in a dream and he turned out to be nice. What are the chances? It would have been so much easier if he was an absolute dick and I spent ages trying to make him be what I wanted him to be, but no. He had to be nice. FML.

'I'm not that hungry,' I mumble, scanning the enormous menu. I can't even seem to read anything. I force myself to slow

down, put my finger on the 'fries' section. There are seven different types of fries. It shouldn't be so hard to choose fries. 'I think
I'm just going to get the "diner fries".'

'You can't just get fries!' he says, from behind his menu. 'You
got meatloaf last time, right? Was it good? If I get that will you
share it with me?' His face pops up over the menu again. He looks
open and eager and happy. It's such a good face. I don't know if
I'll be able to eat anything at all – my stomach's churning – but
I tell him yes, that sounds perfect.

✳

'So have you had any news? About your stepdad?' Dan asks, once
our drinks have arrived, along with some nuts for the table.

I nod. 'It's not good. He's been stealing from the business
for ages, apparently. He's borrowed against my mum's house – I
mean, it was their house, but—' I stop as I see something out of
the corner of my eye, outside the restaurant. It can't have been,
but… I lean forward and peer out of the window.

'Are you OK?' I hear Dan ask. 'What's happening?'

I squint. Standing by a bike rack, waiting to cross the road,
is, I'm pretty sure, Anthony.

'Bea?' Dan says.

'Sorry, I'm just…' I shuffle closer to the window so I can get
a better view next time he turns his head. He's looking left. He
looks right and I'm up and on my feet and moving out of the
restaurant before I even think.

The road is busy, so Anthony's still standing there and as I get
closer I notice he's taken out his phone and is glancing between
the screen and the street. I have no idea what I'm going to say,
but I know I have to say something. He disappeared once and
there's no way I'm going to let him disappear again.

'Anthony,' I say, once I'm almost level with him.

He looks at me and I see confusion flicker across his face.

'Hey,' he says. He smiles. 'Hi.'

He looks exactly the same. He glances back down at his phone and then at the road again.

'How's things?' he says, still smiling. I can't believe he's smiling at me, like he didn't just fuck off and never contact me again.

I stare at him. Actually, he doesn't quite look the same. His blue eyes – the first thing I noticed about him – are small and underlined with bags. His skin is sallow and his forehead is either sweaty or greasy: strands of his dark hair are sticking to it. And then I realise something.

'You have no idea who I am, do you?'

'Um,' he says, glancing left, back down to his phone, and then finally at me. 'I'm sorry, I—'

I laugh. 'It's fine. It's absolutely fine.'

'I meet a lot of people,' he says. 'With work and—'

'No,' I say. 'It's fine, really. It was good to see you anyway. Have a nice life.'

And then I turn back towards the diner.

Why did I ever think he was a loss? Why did I ever waste even one minute wondering about him, trying to work out what I'd done wrong, trying to think if there was anything I could have done to stop him doing what he did? He actually did me a favour. And I am an idiot. Or I was. I'm not any more.

*

'Who was that?' Dan asks, as soon as I sit down.

'Sorry,' I say, reaching for my drink and guzzling some down. I felt completely confident while I was talking to Anthony, but now I'm shaking. 'Ex-boyfriend. Dickhead. Sorry I just walked out.'

'No, that's OK. I was watching in case you needed me.'

'You're so lovely,' I say. I have to tell him. I shake my head to try to clear my thoughts. My mind is racing with memories of Anthony; panting away on top of me in bed while not caring how it was for me, never phoning when he said he was going to, standing me up when I was planning to introduce him to Freya. The time we went to the theatre – to a play he said he wanted to see – and he left partway through without even telling me. I thought he'd gone to the loo and got worried when he didn't come back. After the show, when there was no sign of him anywhere, I texted him and he replied *Soz. Tired.*

I can't believe I've been thinking about him – wondering what happened – for so long. What a waste. I can't make that mistake again.

'Dan,' I say. 'I need to tell you—'

I'm interrupted by the waitress bringing our food. I'd forgotten how fast this place is. She puts my fries down in front of me and the meatloaf – and onion rings – in front of Dan.

'Could we have another plate, please?' Dan asks her. 'We're going to share.'

He smiles at me and the waitress smiles at me and I feel like absolute shit.

*

We've finished the food and I still haven't managed to tell him. I've missed half of the stuff he's said because my brain has just been swimming with the words I need to say to him, getting louder and louder.

'Want to go and get a drink in Covent Garden?' he says, once we've paid.

Again, he looks so bright and enthusiastic and I can't say no. I should tell him now, here. I should tell him and go straight to the Tube. I can be in my bedroom watching something comforting – *Moonstruck*, maybe – in half an hour, if I'm lucky.

'Sounds good,' I say, like a fool.

We walk up Neal Street and pass the shop where Dan bought me socks last time we were here. Anxiety curls in my stomach. I have to tell him tonight.

'Before I moved to London,' I say, as we walk, 'I read something about Covent Garden in a book or a magazine – I can't remember where – and I had this picture of it in my head: a square, surrounded by tall buildings, reddish buildings. At least one of them was a hotel – it had an awning out front, you know? Quite fancy?'

Dan nods.

'And in the middle of the square were benches and flowerbeds, grassy areas—'

'Like the square where we met?' Dan says.

I wince. 'Kind of. And then in the middle was a stone fountain. I think it was a flower. A tulip or a rose? Petals anyway. And the water coming up from the middle. I don't know where I got this image from, but that's the picture in my head even now when I hear Covent Garden. But it doesn't exist. I made it up.'

Dan laughs. 'That's brilliant. I wonder how you came up with it.'

'I don't know,' I tell him. 'But it makes me a bit sad because I always want to go there. Even now, sometimes I'll think to myself "Ooh, I'll go and spend the day in Covent Garden. Sit in the square with a book…" And then I remember that I can't.'

'Well, you can still come to Covent Garden,' he says, as we cross Long Acre by the Tube. 'It's pretty cool.'

'It is,' I say. 'I love the market.'

'I brought my parents here last Christmas,' Dan says. 'My mum was in her element. Thought I'd have to pick her up and carry her back to the hotel.'

I smile at him. 'My mum loves it here too.'

'We should get them both to come down here one weekend. We could introduce them.'

I can't let this go on any longer. If I don't end it now, Dan will invite his mum down and I won't be able to say anything and then I'll have to invite mine and they'll love each other and I won't be able to say anything, and the next thing I'll be standing at the altar, wearing trainers under my wedding dress, and looking for a Fed-Ex truck and Richard Gere.

'Dan…' I say, stopping. We're almost at the bottom of James Street. The market building is just in front of us. It's busy – people are swerving around where we've caused a standing hazard in the middle of the street – and tourists are stopping to take photos of one of those living statues: a man painted gold and sitting in mid-air. A busker on the corner starts to play: Van Morrison's 'Someone Like You'.

If this was a romcom, this would be the moment for a romantic declaration. Dan would get down on one knee maybe and everyone would gather round to watch, cameras at the ready. Or I would tell him that he was the man of my dreams, that I couldn't live without him, and everyone would applaud, even the statue. But no. That's not what I've got to say. Not even close. Someone like you. But not you. Oh god.

'Dan,' I say again. 'You're really great.'

He's still smiling at me. As if he has no idea what's coming. This is why people chicken out. This is why they start to break up with someone and can't go through with it. But I picture Anthony, not even recognising me, even though I look basically the same. I think I might even have the same coat. And I think about Henry looking at me that night with his dark eyes and his long eyelashes. And I think about being in bed with Dan and how wrong it felt. And I take a deep breath and I say, 'I'm really sorry.'

CHAPTER THIRTY-THREE

'How did he take it?' Freya asks.

I got home to find Freya and Georgie on the sofa watching *DIY SOS*. Georgie was in tears (at the show) and Freya was mainlining Doritos.

'He was… surprised,' I tell them, pulling off my shoes and curling up in the armchair. 'Disappointed.'

'But he was OK about it?' Freya asks, glancing at me and then back to the screen.

'Yeah. He was fine. He's a nice bloke.'

I watch the TV for a bit, but my mind drifts back to Covent Garden. Dan's face had dropped when I told him. He looked like a puppy. A kicked puppy. I came close to telling him it was a joke ('Haha! Did you think I was serious? Your face!') but instead, we hugged quickly and I legged it to the Tube. I looked back when I got there – I'd half-worried that he'd come and get the same Tube and we'd have to wait awkwardly on the platform together – but he'd already been swallowed up by the crowd.

The voiceover in my head was in full effect on the way home. Not only telling me everything that had just happened, but also playing 'All By Myself' at full volume. I bought a bottle of wine on the way back from the station in the hope that that would drown it out long enough for me to get to sleep.

'I saw Anthony,' I say now, as Georgie wails 'These people are so good!' at the TV.

'What?' Freya says, turning her entire body towards me. 'Seriously?'

I nod. 'He was outside the restaurant, waiting to cross the road.'

'So you didn't speak to him.'

'I did. I went outside as soon as I saw him – I didn't plan it. I just saw him and the next thing I knew I was on my way out the door.' I picture his face. How I knew that he didn't remember me. All the pain I used to associate with him has just… gone.

'Wow. Good for you. And?'

'He didn't remember me.'

Freya's mouth literally drops open. I'm not sure I've ever seen that happen before. 'What? The fuck?'

I smile, remembering. 'I know. I think maybe I was familiar and he couldn't quite place me? But I'm not even confident of that. And he didn't look good.'

'God,' she says. 'I'm sorry.'

Georgie is wiping her face on her sleeves. Freya drops an arm around her shoulder and pulls her closer.

'It was the best thing that could've happened, to be honest,' I say. 'It made me realise that a) he was a dick, and b) I shouldn't still be thinking about him. Ever.'

'I mean, I told you,' Freya says.

'I know you did.'

'And I was right.'

'You were right.' I smile.

'Shut up, babe,' Georgie says, nuzzling into Freya's neck. 'Bea's epiphany is more important than your ego.'

Freya pulls a face at me over the top of Georgie's head and then kisses her temple.

*

I lie down on the bed and stare up at the stained ceiling. I think I might actually ask Freya to help me decorate in here. I'm going to be here for a while so I don't know why I'm putting up with a boring, bland room when I could have it look however I like. I think a sort of dusky pink might be nice? Maybe with some neon lights like the one in the coffee shop I went to with Dan. Like Demi Moore's apartment in *St Elmo's Fire* but without the Billy Idol wall decal and nervous breakdown.

I sit up and look around. Or maybe Renée Zellweger's apartment in *Down With Love*. White but with a pink padded headboard. Maybe a pink chair in the corner, next to the bookcase Henry made for me. And a fluffy rug. And Freya and Mum have both sold me on chandeliers. I squint and try to picture it. I could put some pictures up too. And get the stuck-on mirror removed and have a big fancy one, leaning up against the wall. It could look great.

It's too early to sleep and my mind's too busy to read so I open up my laptop and try to find a film. Actually, *Down With Love* feels pretty appropriate after the day I've had. Plus it's hilarious and adorable and I haven't watched it for ages.

It opens with a quote about how New York is the place where dreams come true and I roll my eyes. This was meant to take my mind off Dan, not bring him right back. But I know I did the right thing. I should have done it a while ago. But it's hard to let go of a dream.

CHAPTER THIRTY-FOUR

Even reflected in my crap, slightly warped mirror, the dress from Mum's shop looks incredible. I've never seen myself look like this before. I have a lot of favourite clothes and I've had things I've fallen in love with before now, but nothing like this. I watch myself turn in the mirror and the dress swings around me. I laugh out loud.

There's a knock at the door and I call out, 'Hang on!'

Although it's not as if I'm going to change back into my sweats before opening the door, I had imagined presenting myself in this dress, not someone just walking in. But whoever it is obviously didn't hear me anyway because the door opens and Henry takes a couple of steps inside, before stopping dead.

'Hi,' I say. 'Sorry, I was just trying this on. Mum bought it for me. From her shop. You know the one I was telling you about? Where she's been working?'

I'm babbling again. Henry, however, is silent. He looks stunned. Like the salmon in the window of the fishmonger's on the high street.

'What's wrong?' I say, panic crawling up my stomach. What if something's happened to Mum? Or Matt? Or Tom?

'You…' he says, but it comes out as more of a croak. He lifts his arms as if he's going to reach out for me and then drops them at his sides again. 'You look…'

'Oh.' The panic in my belly has gone, but it's been replaced by something else. Something that feels like butterflies. I look down at myself.

'I know. It's gorgeous, isn't it? I can't believe it.'

He shakes his head. 'You look amazing. Are you, uh, going somewhere with Dan? I thought Freya said you'd seen him already.'

'I have,' I say. 'We went out for dinner. And I ended it with him.'

Henry's mouth drops open again. 'Seriously? How come?'

I feel weird having this conversation standing in the middle of the room in my glorious dress. I perch on the edge of the bed. Henry stays standing.

'It wasn't right. It never was. I was totally kidding myself.'

'Because of the dream?'

'Pretty much, yeah. Or, no. Maybe at first. But also because I thought I wanted security. Like Mum had with Tom. But look how that turned out. And also Freya thinks I was trying to protect myself because Anthony was such a nightmare.' What is it with the babbling? How do I stop?

'I'm sorry,' Henry says. 'That sucks.'

'Yeah,' I say. 'I mean, it's for the best. But… yeah.'

He stares at me for a second and I can't work out the expression on his face.

'What are you watching?' he asks, eventually, gesturing at my laptop.

'*Down With Love.*'

He laughs. 'Appropriate.'

'I thought so. Hey, did you want something?'

He looks confused.

'What did you come in here for?'

'Oh right, yeah. *Inception*'s on. I was going to ask if you wanted to watch it.'

'With you?'

'Course. Freya and Georgie've gone out.'

'Even though you've seen it how many times?'

He grins. 'A few. But I haven't seen it for a while. I don't let myself rewatch it very often so it keeps its effect.'

'Oh god. OK. I'll get changed. Have we got any popcorn or anything?'

'I'll go and have a look.'

He's almost out of the room when I add, 'And beer.'

*

'I don't understand it,' I say after about five minutes.

While I was getting changed, Henry went out and bought popcorn and beer, plus chocolate and biscuits and olives and cheese and ham. ('I didn't know what you fancied.')

'You have to stick with it,' he says. 'It'll be explained in a bit. Sort of.'

'Still don't get it,' I say after fifteen minutes, when I'm frowning so hard my forehead is sore and I've eaten a full bowl of popcorn. And it's about dreams. I mean, I knew that, but I'd forgotten. Why won't the universe let me not think about bloody dreams for five bloody minutes?

'He explains it in a bit,' Henry says. 'Ish.'

I like the bit where Paris folds up and Ellen Page does the thing with the mirrors, but I still have no clue what's going on. Not even when Leonardo explains it.

'What do you like about this film exactly?' I ask Henry, after about an hour. I still don't really understand what's going on, but I'm on my second beer and I'm letting it wash over me. And I've eaten all the cheese (and most of the olives).

'I like the characters. And their dynamic. And the concept.'

I don't particularly like the characters. And I can't say I think much to their dynamic either. But the concept is cool, I'll give him that. It would've been interesting to read, like, a paragraph about.

'How long is it?' I ask him.

'Um,' he says, shuffling on the sofa. 'About two and a half hours, I think.'

Oh sweet Jesus. I open another beer.

*

I'm in the park. The sun is shining and I feel warm and safe and happy. I see someone in the distance, walking towards me, but the sun's in my eyes and I can't tell who it is. I know though. I know without even seeing him.

I keep walking and he keeps walking and then we both stop. And smile.

'Hey,' Henry says. 'Fancy seeing you here.'

And then I wake up.

*

I wake up on the sofa with my head on Henry's shoulder. I don't know that at first. Not exactly. At first I'm not quite sure where I am or who I'm with, but eventually I realise I'm on the sofa, my head's on Henry's shoulder, there's a crick in my neck and I must've let go of a beer 'cos I'm sitting in a wet patch. I hope that's why, anyway. My arm's against Henry's arm. My thigh's pressed up against Henry's thigh. I feel warm all down that side. (And wet down the other side, which I could live without.)

I move away slowly and realise that Henry's asleep too. His glasses have slipped down his nose and his long eyelashes are fluttering as he dreams. I look over at the TV. Bloody *Inception* is still on – is it the film that never ends?

As I shift on the sofa, a beer bottle rolls away from my leg, so at least I was right about the puddle. That's a relief. I put it on the table and grab another olive, before looking back at Henry. He looks good asleep. Some people don't. Some people sleep with their mouths open, grunting. I've seen them on the train. But Henry looks peaceful. His mouth is closed, and I can see a tiny patch of stubble under his bottom lip. His haircut definitely suits him too. His fringe is sort of soft and brushing his eyebrows and—

He opens his eyes. And catches me staring at him. Shit.

'Sorry,' I say, flustered, shifting further back on the sofa.

He blinks at me. 'I fell asleep?'

'You did.' I don't think I need to tell him that I did too.

He pushes his glasses up his nose and peers at the TV. 'The film's still on.'

'I think it's on forever now. We just have to get used to it.'

'What time is it?'

I pull my phone out of my pocket. 'Eleven.'

'Shit,' he says. 'Better get to bed.'

'Yeah.' I don't move. I'm sitting in a wet patch.

He's still looking at me and I guess I'm still looking back at him. And then he stands up suddenly.

'Night,' he says, rubbing one hand back through his hair. The new soft fringe falls back down over his forehead.

'Sweet dreams,' I say. Like a dickhead.

CHAPTER THIRTY-FIVE

At work the next day, Henry seems different. More relaxed. I'd almost describe him as chirpy. He made us teas when we first came in and I think I heard him whistling in the kitchen. I'm not sure I've ever heard him whistle before.

I'm actually feeling pretty chirpy myself. Ending things with Dan has turned out to be an enormous weight off my shoulders. Which seems outrageous when I think about how long I spent longing for him, wanting to meet him, actually looking for him. But I haven't even dreamt about him for ages. I dreamt about Henry last night.

I smile to myself as I unpack a box of books. There's an historical romance by one of my favourite authors and I put it to one side to read later (although the cover features a blindfolded woman in a very low-cut dress with boobs like basketballs perched on top, so maybe I'll save it to read at home).

Henry brings out teas and he's definitely whistling. Although he stops when he sees me.

'You hungry?' he says.

I had a piece of toast before we left home, but I could definitely eat. 'What were you thinking?'

'Bacon sarnie?'

I pull a face at him. We're not allowed to eat hot food in the shop. We have occasionally broken that rule, but bacon has a pretty strong smell, so if someone from head office came in—

'Live a little,' Henry says, picking up the book I just put down, before turning bright pink and dropping it again.

'Go on then,' I say. 'With ketchup please.'

'Excellent,' he says, heading for the door. 'Will you be all right on your own?'

'I think I'll manage,' I say, smiling. But he's already gone.

*

We have one of the best days we've had in the shop for a while. First the bacon sandwiches and more tea – no one from head office turns up, thank god – and then a preschool group comes in to choose a picture book each and the children run riot. But in a cute way. I end up sitting on the floor reading *I Am Not Sleepy and I Will Not Go To Bed* to a little girl who is definitely sleepy, even though it's early afternoon, and a boy who has his finger up his nose the entire time.

Once they've gone, we put Radio 2 back on and tidy and clean the shop, singing along to Steve Wright's oldies. Henry shows me how singing along with the radio makes you feel like you're in a music video, by miming while posing moodily around the shop – leaning against a bookshelf, pretending to be engrossed in a book, at the desk with my phone held up to his ear – and I laugh so much I come very close to wetting my pants.

We lock up and walk home together, stopping at the grocer's for some vegetables, spices and mixed beans for the curry Henry's planning to make.

'Did you finish watching that film?' Henry asks me, as he passes me a bag of spinach and I drop it in the basket.

'*Inception*? Fuck no.'

He laughs, looking down at the recipe he printed off the internet. 'No, not that. The one you were watching in your room. When you were… trying on your dress?'

He's gone pink.

'Oh! *Down With Love*. No. But I've seen it before. Why?'

'Have we got ginger or garlic at home?' He's still staring at the printout.

'Maybe. But you'd better get some anyway, just in case. So why? *Down With Love?*'

'Oh.' He throws a bag of garlic to me and I put it in the basket. 'I was going to say I'd watch it with you. Since you watched *Inception* with me.'

'I mean, not much of it. I fell asleep. And before that I just complained about how it didn't make sense. Didn't you say you needed an onion?'

He checks and nods, so I put one in the basket.

'Well yeah. But still. You watched my film, I think it's only fair for me to watch yours.'

'Have you got a thing for Renée Zellweger? Does Reese know?'

'Can you grab a tin of coconut milk?' he says, picking up a head of broccoli and two enormous, gnarled sweet potatoes. 'And no. I just thought about what you said at brunch that day. About men and romcoms. I feel like I've dismissed them for no good reason. And I'm ready for you to teach me their ways.'

'Is this because you loved *Notting Hill?*'

'I did love *Notting Hill*,' he says. 'Beans.'

The beans are just along from the coconut milk so I grab them both and say, 'Is that it?'

'Just…' He scans over the recipe again, his brow furrowed. 'Cashew nuts and a lime.'

'Perfect,' I say. 'And then *Down With Love* for dessert.'

✳

We watch the film on my laptop. On my bed. Henry's arm is warm against mine, our hips bump whenever we shift position. There's a horrendously awkward few minutes when the film's main characters are pantomiming sex over split screens and Henry and I both drink almost all of our beers to cover our embarrassment, but he loves the film and doesn't get up to leave when it ends.

'I need to tell you something,' Henry says, as I close the laptop and push it further down the bed.

I shift slightly so I can look at him and he moves back a little too, turning towards me.

'Is it something bad?' I ask. I'm suddenly terrified that his dad's selling the flat or Henry's planning to leave the bookshop. There have been too many changes, endings, lately, I can't take another.

'No. I mean, I hope not. Maybe?' He blows out a breath. 'Fuck. I need another beer.'

'Want me to get you one?'

He shakes his head, his eyes closed. 'No. I'm good. I just need to…' He looks at me. His eyes look dark. He takes another breath. 'I think… I think I'm in love with you.'

'What?' I say, brilliantly.

He nods. 'I think, yeah. I think I have been for… a while.'

'How long?' I ask, as if that's an important question. As if it matters at all.

He rubs one hand over his face. 'I don't know exactly. I mean, I fancied you right from the start. When you walked into the shop, I was just…' He picks up his beer and swigs it. 'I knew I was going to give you the job before you even said a word.'

'What? Henry!'

'I know,' he says, half-smiling. 'So unprofessional. But it worked out great! You're good at it. I knew you would be.'

'Is that why you offered me the room too?' I ask. This room. The room we're sitting in now, having this utterly surreal conversation.

'Um.' He drinks some more beer. 'Would it be bad if I said yes?'

'Oh my god.' I laugh. 'Oh my god, Henry!'

'I know. I'm sorry. Are you freaking out? Do you want me to lie? No, that's not why I offered you the room.'

I close my eyes and try to breathe. Henry has liked me since the very start. That's why I got the job. That's why I live in this house. Everything I have right now, I have because Henry liked me.

'So?' Henry says. He sounds nervous. 'Bea? I didn't offer you the job or the house because I fancied you, I promise. I knew you'd be great at the job. And then you needed somewhere to say. I know it sounds creepy—'

'It sounds a bit creepy,' I say.

He nods. 'That's why I never told you. Freya said—'

'Freya knows?!'

'Yeah. She kind of… guessed. And then beat it out of me.'

'I can't believe Freya knows.'

'Adam and Celine don't know. I don't think.'

'Well that's a relief.'

'So. What do you think?'

'God. Well, first of all I'm in no position to judge since I moved here to find a person who doesn't exist. And I hung around the park and asked out a random man and then broke his heart.'

'You broke his heart?'

'No. I don't know. Shut up. I'm trying to think.'

'Sorry.'

After a few seconds, I ask him the most pressing question. 'How did you know?'

'Oh,' he says, shuffling on the bed again. 'OK, well, when you introduced me to Dan, you called me your landlord and work colleague and friend. In that order.'

Shit. 'I didn't mean—'

He holds his hands up. 'No, it's fine. I know you didn't. But the way it made me feel… I realised I wanted you to say "boyfriend". I honestly hadn't realised until right that moment. I don't think. I mean, I knew I liked you. But hearing you introduce me like that was when I knew it wasn't enough. And it would never be enough.'

'Henry.'

'And then you said you'd had a panic attack. And I thought about you there on your own. I know you weren't on your own. I know Dan was with you and he took care of you. But I couldn't stand the thought of it. Of you being scared. And then I couldn't stand the thought of him taking care of you. I started thinking about what it would be like if the two of you were really serious. If he really was your dream man. And I knew I couldn't take it. I felt like it was suffocating me.'

'I'm sorry.'

He smiles. 'It's not your fault.'

I think back about all the time we've spent together. In the shop and at home. Brunch at Mr C's. All the Adam bonus dinners. Henry building me a bookshelf. I can't imagine my life without him in it. I don't want to.

❧

'So what do you think?' Henry says. He's biting his thumbnail, sliding it between his front teeth. I think about the splinter. Holding his hand. His stomach when he pulled out his knackered old T-shirt.

'I think…' I say. And then I lean forward and brush my lips across his. My eyes are still open, but he closes his, his long eyelashes brushing his cheeks. I can see the little frown line between his eyebrows and I want to smooth it out with my thumb, or kiss it away. I slide my hand around the back of his neck, my fingers up into his hair.

I thought it would be weird, kissing Henry, after being friends for so long, but it's not weird at all. It feels good. It feels right.

His hands move around my waist and I let myself relax against him, my chest pressing against his. I feel him sigh against my mouth, and I part my lips, my tongue grazing his bottom lip, slipping into his mouth. He opens his mouth, deepening the kiss, and I finally close my eyes.

With Dan, when we kissed, I couldn't make my brain be quiet. With Henry, I feel like I'm underwater. Or floating in space. Everything is dark, warm, velvety. And then the blackness is interrupted with bursts of light.

Fireworks.

CHAPTER THIRTY-SIX

The following morning I'm making a coffee in the kitchen when Henry comes in. He's in his pyjama bottoms and holey T-shirt and I want to slide my hands up underneath it and touch his skin.

'Morning,' he says, his voice still croaky with sleep.

I smile at him. 'Morning.'

He didn't stay in my room. Not all night anyway. He stayed for a while. And we kissed so much that my lips felt sore and swollen, and my cheeks hurt from smiling. I didn't sleep much, but when I did I dreamt about him. Not in the park though. Everywhere. And then I woke up stupidly early, showered and dressed and came downstairs to make breakfast.

'Picnic today,' he says, pressing up against me.

I tip my head back and he kisses me, his hands curving around my neck, fingers pressing into my hair. I want him to lift me up on the countertop and pull my dress up over my head.

'Missed you,' he says against my mouth.

I laugh. 'Shut up.'

'Can't believe I get to kiss you,' he says, dragging his lips along my jaw.

I slide my hands under his T-shirt and dig my thumbs into his waist. He wriggles under my hands. Ticklish.

'Oh. My. God,' I hear Freya say.

I lean back from Henry's kiss and peep at her over his shoulder. She's wearing a black lace bralette and red satin football shorts. I'm not even going to ask.

'Don't turn round,' I tell Henry. 'She's barely dressed.'

He drops his forehead down on my shoulder as Freya scoffs. 'Prude. You two deserve each other.' She grins. 'Actually, you really do.' She crosses the kitchen, bumping a chair out of her way with her hip and wraps her arms around us both. 'So happy you finally worked it out.'

'Thanks.' I grin at her.

She reaches up and musses Henry's hair. 'And so glad I don't have to keep not telling her your guilty secret.'

'Thanks,' Henry tells her without turning around. 'You were a great help.'

He turns his head so his lips brush my neck and I gasp.

'Oh fucking hell, not in the kitchen,' Freya says. 'Pubes on the counter are way worse than dishes in the sink.'

'Oh my god, Freya!' I say.

As she leaves the room, I hear her yell, 'Adam! Celine! Don't go in the kitchen! Bea and Henry are getting it on.'

'Yes!' Adam bellows. 'Fucking finally!'

Followed by the sound of Celine vomiting.

*

The sun is shining and Celine's brought picnic blankets and a big plastic sheet. She's so organised.

'What do you think of this one?' she asks, passing me some Rightmove details she's printed off the internet. It's a four bed semi with enormous rooms and original fireplaces in the living room and bedrooms, plus subway tile in the kitchen. I love subway tile.

'It's lovely,' I tell her, as I flick through the photos. 'No garden though.' Just a big paved yard.

'Yeah, that's what I was thinking. Adam says it's near a park, but I think a garden would be lovely.' She leans back on her arms and shifts her bum on the picnic blanket. She's got piles. She's been telling me. Even though I've asked her not to. I pass the printout to Freya.

The next one is an end terrace with smaller rooms, fireplaces, a beautiful kitchen and a balcony off the bedroom, plus a big garden.

'This one's great,' I say, passing it to Freya. 'What's wrong with it?'

Celine glances at Adam, who's fiddling with the barbecue. 'Close to Adam's mum.'

'There's nothing wrong with my mum,' Adam says without looking up. 'She's a wonderful woman.'

'Oh she is,' Celine says, shaking her head at me and Freya. 'But I don't want her popping in every sodding day.'

'Yeah,' Adam says, striking a match. 'She would definitely do that.'

Celine rolls the printout up and passes it to Adam. 'You can light the barbecue with this, hon.'

'Hon?' Freya says, reaching for the next printout.

'It's the hormones,' Celine says.

The next property's not much to look at from the outside, and the bathroom and kitchen need updating, but there's a big garden and it's a hundred grand less than the other two.

'Adam likes that one,' Celine says. 'Reckons he's going to do it up himself.'

'Oh god no,' Freya says.

'Oi,' Adam says, shaking the box of matches in our direction. 'I am man. I can make fire. I can renovate kitchen.'

'You can't even change a lightbulb,' Celine says. 'He always breaks the fitting.'

'True,' Adam says, flopping down next to her and resting his head on her lap. 'But I can get a man in.' He turns his head towards her torso and says, 'Hello, baby!' in a ridiculous voice.

'Stop talking to my vagina,' Celine says, running her fingers through his hair.

I look at the two of them together and realise that if they'd come into the shop a few months ago, Henry and I would have guessed wrong. We'd have said 'split'; that they were too different, they bicker too much, he's too rough and it annoys her and she's shrill and dismissive. But we'd have been wrong. Because despite their differences, they love each other. And despite the way they used to, and sometimes still do, come across in public, they're properly there for each other when it counts. Which is much more important than how their relationship looks to a couple of bored, nosy booksellers.

'Have you showed them my fave?' Adam asks, still curled up with Celine.

'No,' Celine says. 'Because it's bollocks.'

'Show them,' he says.

'Show us,' I copy.

She passes me the printout. It's a two bedroom penthouse. With a huge terrace, a bar and red leopard-patterned wallpaper in the bedroom.

'This is bollocks,' I say, rolling it up and smacking Adam on the head with it.

He rolls off Celine's lap. 'It's my dream.'

'And has been since this very morning,' Celine says. 'If I was going to live in a penthouse, it wouldn't be in bloody Southend.'

'This disparagement of Southend has to stop,' Adam says. 'It's not good for the baby.' He sits up. 'Oi oiiiiii! Here comes Henry.'

He's been for more beer.

※

The burgers smell incredible, but I can also smell the deli over the road: garlic, tomatoes, coffee. And the fumes from the traffic. My favourite smell. The smell of my life in London.

I look around. At Celine and Adam, who are nuzzling each other and giggling. It's kind of disturbing, but also really sweet. At Freya, who is inevitably on her phone, but who glances up and grins at me, one eyebrow raised. At Henry, who is pressed right up against me, his hand resting on my thigh, his chin on my shoulder as his lips graze my jaw.

I remember when I Googled dreams coming true and read the suggestion that dreams just tell you what you really know – or feel – about something, but haven't consciously recognised. I think that's true. My subconscious knew Henry was the one for me before I did. I saw him in my dreams before I really saw him in real life.

And I finally realise, it was never about Dan. About the man in the dream. I was looking for the wrong thing the whole time. The dream – the feeling of love and warmth and comfort it gave me – was about this. Me. Here. With my friends. With Henry.

I tip my head back and he kisses me. And it's slow and gentle and soft and sweet. And our teeth don't clash and our noses don't bump and I know that he is mine. He is meant for me.

He's the man of my dreams.

A LETTER FROM KERIS

I want to say a huge thank you for choosing to read *It Had to Be You*. If you did enjoy it, and want to keep up to date with all my latest releases, just sign up at the following link. Your email address will never be shared and you can unsubscribe at any time.

www.bookouture.com/keris-stainton

I hope you loved *It Had to Be You* and if you did I would be very grateful if you could write a review. I'd love to hear what you think, and it makes such a difference helping new readers to discover one of my books for the first time.

I love hearing from my readers – you can get in touch on my Facebook page, through Twitter, Goodreads or my website.

Thanks,
Keris Stainton

 www.keris-stainton.com

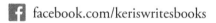 facebook.com/keriswritesbooks

 twitter.com/Keris

ACKNOWLEDGEMENTS

As ever, biggest thanks go to my lovely agent Hannah Sheppard and fabulous editor Abigail Fenton. You get me. (Also you take me to nice places. Thank you for that.)

Thank you to everyone at Bookouture, particularly Emma Rogers for another fabulous cover; Jennie Ayres and Becca Allen for catching all my embarrassing errors, and Kim Nash and Noelle Holten for promo brilliance.

Thanks to Keren David for taking me on a nostalgia tour of East Finchley. It's changed a lot since I lived there and I've mixed the old and new in this book. And some other bits I just totally made up. (Those battered aubergines are real though, and you should try them if you get the chance. They're from Majjo's on Fortis Green.) To the real Mrs C (who is almost certainly no longer with us), thank you for always being lovely (and for the free food).

Thanks to Craig Stevens for the discount bookshop info (all mistakes and made up stuff my own, obvs) – hope you like your cameo. To the various bookshops I worked in years ago and the creepy customers for all the anecdotes. To Jenni Nock for Henry's reasons for liking *Inception*. To Katy Walker for tax tips (again, any errors are my own). To my Facebook friends for sexy accountancy puns, the correct word for the tip-up trolley wheelie thing (which I ignored) and for generally keeping me entertained while I avoid writing. And to Sarah Watkins for the lunch at The Diner that lasted till dinner.

To all my group chat faves – I don't know what I'd do without you. Apart from a lot more work. A special shout out to Aimee, Andi, Doris, Heather, Helen, Jo, Lesley, Trac and Vivi. Thank you to the wise and wonderful Mollusks for your insightful comments on romcoms, bad boyfriends, adorable boybands and more. To the Adult Lady Fans of One Direction Slack – particularly Ally and Nora for setting it up – you are my happy place. And I couldn't not mention my romcoms-on-Netflix-loving muse, Harry Styles.

Finally, as always, all the love to Team Stainto, my little shipmates.

Made in the USA
Coppell, TX
17 May 2021

Twenty-five-year-old **Bea** is a hopeless romantic – with a hopeless love life. She's been single ever since her awful ex broke her heart, and the only thing she gets up to in bed is watching rom coms on her laptop.

When Bea meets **Dan**, who is basically *the man of her dreams*, she knows she can't let him get away. They might not have fireworks, but not everyone can be fighting and (loudly) making up every night, like Bea's housemates.

But Bea can't shift the feeling that something just isn't *right*. As time goes on, Dan seems less like Mr Right, and more like Mr Couldn't-Be-More-Wrong… Will Bea be brave enough to change her dreams – and dare to ask for more?

A laugh-out-loud tale for anyone who's ever dreamt of a fairy-tale romance and found a real-life happy ending, for fans of Giovanna Fletcher, Cate Woods, and Mhairi McFarlane.

www.bookouture.com

ISBN 9781786812902

90000 >

9 781786 812902